Fire

David West

ACKNOWLEDGEMENTS

Once again I would like to thank my wife Claire and my editor, Debz Hobbs-Wyatt for their valuable input to this book. Jacqueline Abromeit has again produced a brilliant cover design. I also wish to thank my friend John, since a philosophical debate on a long walk inspired an important theme of this book.

PROLOGUE

It was a little before midnight on Saint Benedict's Day, 1607. A thick layer of stratus cloud dimmed and diffused the faint light of a crescent moon. A horse harnessed to a cart was grazing on the verge in a side street. The cart was illuminated by flickering light emerging from an open door at the side of the twelfth-century church of Santa Giustina, in the picturesque town of Monselice, south of Padua. Two men stood warming their hands around the fire in the apse. Their faces glowed red in the firelight.

'When the fat burns, it really gets going, doesn't it, Roti?'

'Yes, master.'

'If the next priest is as fat as this one, I don't think we'll need to waste as much brandy getting it going, do you?'

'No, master.'

'What are you doing?'

'The silver-jewelled crucifix. No point leaving it, master. If I can get near enough and hook it off him with this shovel, I think I can reach it. I forgot to take it off him, in all the excitement.'

'Watch out, you oaf! You've messed up the earth bund I made. Forget the crucifix and use your shovel to put the bund back as it was. Be quick about it, we mustn't linger, satisfying as it is.'

PART ONE

CHAPTER ONE

He went in and closed the door behind him. His uncle did not look up from his writing, but signalled with his left hand that the visitor should sit in the chair in front of his large desk. Pietro sat and while his uncle continued to write, he looked around the room. Two works of Giorgio Vasari graced the wall to his left. The nearest, The Entombment, depicted the disciples carrying the lifeless Christ to his tomb. It was a dark work, beautifully executed, but with a minimum of colour. Pietro much preferred the further painting, The Garden of Gethsemane. There was more colour. He was attracted to the vibrant red, yellow and gold robes of the two male disciples, asleep in the foreground. Their slumbering bodies formed a vee shape, within which Mary Magdalene also slept, her head resting on her left hand. Above Mary, Christ was praying, his arms outstretched. A winged-cherub held out a gold chalice towards him. Christ was adorned in red and blue, exquisitely detailed folds of cloth. He found something about the vee shape, framing Mary, exciting. There was only one work on the wall to his right, Salome with the Head of John the Baptist, by Titian. His attention was drawn back to the desk as his uncle signed the paper with a flourish, and then put down his quill. He focussed on the paper, as his uncle looked up, but his uncle then turned the paper, and pressed it against the leather-bound blotting pad, leaving it there upside-down.

'Pietro, thank you for coming to visit me. How is my favourite nephew?' He felt his uncle's hazel eyes drilling into his own.

'I am very well, Uncle, and hope that I can be of service.'

'His Holiness, Pope Innocent, is an old and frail man. It is possible that, before long, I may take his place. I have been giving it much thought.'

'Uncle Ippolito, if I can be of any service to you, it would be my honour.'

'God tells me you will be of very great service. I am considering making you and Cinzio cardinals, if I am elected, of course. It will comfort me to know I have the loyalty of my nephews.'

'Speaking for myself, you will forever have my loyalty, Uncle. I'm sure that Cinzio will feel the same.' He took another fleeting glance towards the Garden of Gethsemane. 'If they elect you, Uncle, will you appoint a new Secretary of State?'

'Yes, Pietro. I welcome your thoughts concerning Cinzio. I also expect he will be loyal, but to hear it from you is doubly reassuring. As he is the eldest, it seems only right. I hope you are not disappointed.'

'Of course not, Uncle, but is age everything? As your brother's son, I bear the Aldobrandini name, while, as your sister's son, Cinzio does not.'

'What's in a name? To those distant from Rome, it would look less like nepotism, if I appointed Cinzio to such an important position. I am concerned to be seen to be doing the right thing. We rely so heavily on Spain, their power and their gold.'

'Wouldn't it be better, Uncle, if we did not have to rely on Spain? What about the Venetians and the Genoese, Uncle? Are they not rich and powerful too?'

'You are right, Pietro, but the Venetian strength makes them rebellious. They launch two or three new ships a week, I have been told, but they are our bastion against the Ottomans. The Genoese dance with Spain. Their banks support Philip, and their ships toil for him in the Americas. The Genoese will not cause us much trouble. France would be a glorious prize. I have heard that Henry has found a new mistress, a Catholic, I am told.'

'I could make some investigations for you. I understand that her name is Gabrielle d'Estrées, Uncle. Perhaps I could influence her to convert Henry to the faith. It is presently only English money and German troops that keep Henry in power. His reign is precarious, is it not, Uncle?'

'I may have underestimated you, Pietro. I like your train of thought. It would be reassuring to be less reliant on Spain. In the meantime, however, there is something that we must do for them. You may be able to help.'

'What is it, Uncle Ippolito?'

'There is a man they call the memory man. He is from

Naples. His name is Giordano Bruno. At present, I understand, he is in Frankfurt. The Spanish want him dead, but he knows people, important people, and he can perform incredible feats of memory. They say that he can memorise entire books of the bible. Someone with his contacts, and his memory, would be a valuable resource. I would like you to make a plan. Find some way of enticing him to one of the papal states, where we can have him arrested.'

'What would we arrest him for?'

'He has written several books. They will be in the papal library. If he has written a book, he is almost certain to have committed heresy. You just have to look hard enough.'

'I shall start researching him at once, Uncle. If the Spanish want him dead, I wonder how much they are prepared to pay.'

'I expect that the price will increase, once we have him, and start teasing his knowledge from him.'

'I will begin work on him at once, Uncle. There is another project I have been working on, a lady of interest, Lucrezia d'Este. She is a great patron of the arts, a kindred spirit if you like. She entered into an affair with Count Ercole Contrari, captain of the ducal guard. Her brother, Duke Alfonso, had the count and his sister taken to his palace in Ferrara, and had the count strangled in front of her. She hates her family with a vengeance, Uncle. It is possible that, with her help, we could bring Este within the realm of the papal states.'

'Very good, Pietro, I am more and more certain that I have now chosen the right nephew.'

One year later, on the third of February 1592, Pietro Aldobrandini visited his uncle to kiss his ring.

'Your Holiness, I devote myself anew to your service. The cardinals have made a wise choice.'

'With your help and guidance, they have, Pietro. You shall join their ranks as soon as it is seemly for me to install my nephews.'

'Thank you, Your Holiness. I am intrigued to know why you chose the name Clement for your papacy.'

'Clement the seventh was ambitious, and a great art lover. It was he who commissioned Da Vinci to paint The Last Supper, you know. It just appealed to me. Tell me, how does the business go with the memory man?'

'I have been befriending several Venetians, Your Holiness. Some are less rebellious than others, and I have found a man who envies my art collection, a man named Giovani Mocenigo. Last year, he went to the Frankfurt fair and met the memory man. Mocenigo seems to have fallen under his spell and wants to learn his memory tricks. He has invited him to Venice.'

'Will he go?'

'He covets the chair in mathematics at the University of Padua.'

'It might be embarrassing to arrest a Professor of Padua University; the liberal intellectuals wouldn't like it.'

'There is no need to be concerned. I have made arrangements for another fellow to get it, Galileo Galilei.'

'I haven't heard of him, is he biddable?'

'He should be. His father was an impoverished musician, and he has illegitimate daughters.'

'Good, so you should encourage this Mocenigo to lure the memory man to Venice. Will the Venetians give him up to us?'

'From what I have heard, the fellow will soon wear out his welcome. Mocenigo covets one of my paintings by Caravaggio, I will miss it, but I will do it for you, Uncle, Your Holiness.'

'You will be rewarded, Pietro. I trust you have found suitable crimes to charge him with.'

'You were quite right, Your Holiness, blasphemies riddle his books. He says that every star in the sky is like earth and inhabited.'

'How pleasant to see you again, so soon, Pietro, forgive me, Cardinal Aldobrandini. You bring news perhaps?'

'Yes, Your Holiness, Gabrielle d'Estrées has been successful. Henry wishes to embrace the faith again. He renounces Protestantism.'

'Excellent, make the arrangements. What wonderful news! We shall have an additional, powerful revenue stream, and be less dependent on Spain. He remains without an heir, though. His wife Margaret de Valois retired to the Auvergne, I believe.'

'That is so, Your Holiness. He does, however, have children by his many mistresses. He wishes to have his marriage annulled, and marry Gabrielle.'

'Good, it is not a problem for me.'

'His councillors are against it, and, forgive me, Your Holiness, but it would not go down well with the other cardinals.'

'Meddling, ungrateful, pious bastards. Can't they appreciate how hard I work for Rome?'

'Perhaps I should see if I can find a suitable wife for him, Your Holiness, one who would serve our purposes.'

'Yes, yes, good idea, Pietro.'

'There is something else, Your Holiness. I have been receiving letters from an Englishman, Joseph Creswell, a Jesuit and friend of Robert Persons. Creswell was chaplain to the Duke of Parma's army in Flanders. It concerns the English problem. King Philip has had visitors from Scotland, Hugh Barclay and John Cecil, seeking support. They are agents of the Earls of Erroll, Huntley, and Angus. They say it would be a most dangerous thing to support James the sixth. He is Protestant to the core. If we wish to convert the kingdoms of Scotland and England, then we should lend our support to them, rather than James.'

'England would be a magnificent prize. Keep me informed.'

'Creswell has also been in touch with Robert Bellarmine.'

'Bellarmine, what is his involvement in this?'

'It is supportive, Your Holiness, and we should keep it that way. He has written the definitive book on God's grace, as I'm sure you know. With his help, should you wish to depose a king, it could be because he had acted against God's grace.'

In December 1595, Cardinal Aldobrandini once again visited his uncle, Pope Clement the Eighth in the Quirinal Palace, Rome.

'Your Holiness, I have had further interesting

communication from Creswell. He argues convincingly that in order to establish the Catholic faith in England again, an English, Catholic king is necessary. Unfortunately, the only possibility seems to be to convert King James of Scotland. Yet he is a wild heretic and could upset the political equilibrium of Europe. He also points out that it is dangerous to appoint one king for the entire island. To everybody its soul, and to every ship its pilot.'

'Yes, he has a point. We must bide our time, yet seize the opportunity when it arises.'

On the eighth of May 1598, a procession passed through the great gate, the Porta di San Giorgio, in Ferrara. There were eight hundred men in the procession, and the entire population of the city lined the streets. Provision-laden mules led the cavalcade. They were followed by five mounted officers, ahead of five hundred mounted musketeers and lancers. Behind them rode a long train of pontifical officials and foreign diplomats. Struggling to keep up, four men carried an effigy of Christ under a ceremonial silver canopy. Close behind the swaying effigy of Christ came a column of twenty-seven cardinals, on foot, with three magistrates. The pope's treasurer rode behind the magistrates, tossing specially minted coins into the crowd. The coins commemorated the glorious return to papal rule of the city. Behind him came Pope Clement the Eighth, carried in a sedan chair with eight porters and covered by a canopy of gold cloth. At the rear, Cardinal Pietro Aldobrandini followed in a coach.

On Friday, the fifteenth of February 1600, Cardinal Aldobrandini visited his uncle again.

'Thank you for your report of the trial, Pietro. I agree, I think we have got everything from Bruno, the memory man, that we are going to get. Bellarmine agrees, as does Borghese. Have the Spaniards raised their offer at all?'

'No, Your Holiness. Twenty thousand ducats is all they are prepared to pay for his execution.'

'Well, it's better than nothing, and we should move on. You must have him handed over to the civil authorities for the execution.'

'Yes, Your Holiness.'

In November 1603, Pietro Aldobrandini was summoned to see his uncle again.

'Pietro, you will be proud of me. I put on my best papal persona, and the Englishman bought it hook, line and sinker. I offered to hear his confession, and he told me everything. If he survives the mission we have sent him on, he could be useful to us again.'

'Useful, in what way, Your Holiness?'

'Well, he is more intelligent than he appears. He speaks a multitude of languages, like a native. He is a ferocious and formidable fighter, and he can open any lock without a key. He is also an expert in breaking ciphers. He was taught everything, apart from languages, by the English secret service. He was their best spy, yet he has remained a Catholic. If he survives his mission, I am quite certain he will return to Florence. There is a woman he has fallen in love with, called Francesca. They already have illegitimate children. He won't be able to stay in Florence since he knows that the duke poisoned his brother to take the crown. Keep your eyes out for him. He will either collect his family and take them back to England, or he will come to Rome.'

'I will make it a priority, Your Holiness.'

CHAPTER TWO

On Saturday, the twenty-second of August 1607, two guests were being entertained at the villa of Sir Anthony Standen and his wife, Francesca. Hugh O'Neill, the exiled Earl of Tyrone, had arrived two days earlier, and Cardinal Aldobrandini had arrived only an hour ago. Anthony hadn't seen Hugh since 1599, when he had attempted to enlist in Hugh's rebel Irish army in order to spy on him for the Earl of Essex. He had first met Cardinal Aldobrandini in 1603, when he was carrying news of King James's ascension around Europe. Anthony and Francesca's nineteen-year-old twins, Antonio and Maria, were also at the dining table. Five-year-old William and baby Anna were asleep upstairs. Hugh appeared to Anthony to have aged in the years since they had last met in. He was still tall, an inch taller than Anthony, but stooped just the slightest amount. His ginger hair was fast losing the battle with grey. His moustache still had speckles of ginger, but his long beard was grey.

His tall, broad expanse of forehead was deeply lined. It appeared to Anthony that Cardinal Aldobrandini had hardly changed at all. That oval face of his, and rather disinterested expression, disguised a sharp and ruthless mind.

'This wine is rather good, Sir Anthony,' Cardinal Aldobrandini said, swirling it in his goblet before sipping it again. 'You have done well with the villa and vineyard that we sold you.'

'Thank you, cardinal. That is indeed a compliment, considering the quality of the papal cellars. Perhaps you would like a tour of the vineyard in the morning?'

'Perhaps, if we have time.'

'Excuse me, I think by the smell, that the vegetables are ready,' Francesca said, getting up from the table. 'Maria, Antonio, would you help me carve and bring the meal in, please?' Cardinal Aldobrandini waited until Francesca had taken Antonio and Maria to the kitchen, before leaning across the table towards Anthony and Hugh.

'There have been some thefts from churches, and now two priests have been murdered in the most extraordinary circumstances. We have investigated, of course, but so far we have found nothing to lead us to the culprit.'

'Forgive me, your eminence, but if the resources of the church have failed, what do you think we can do?' Anthony asked.

'The seal of the confession is, of course, sacrosanct. I don't know any details, but on his deathbed, Pope Clement told me that if there were ever a need for unearthing secrets, then we should call on your special talents. I don't know what talents you have, but I think we need them now. We must discover who is responsible, whilst also avoiding panic. I think Earl Hugh and you, Sir Anthony, will make a formidable team. We will, of course, pay handsomely for your services. How do two thousand ducats each sound?'

'What are the extraordinary circumstances of these murders?' Anthony enquired.

'Both priests have been burnt to death, in their churches, with a circle of soil around their bodies.'

'How did they come to be burnt?' Hugh interjected.

'There were some pieces of unburnt straw. We think the murderer must have knocked them unconscious and then tied them onto some bales of straw. He seems to have soaked it in brandy to ensure a swift conflagration. Perhaps the soil was to form some sort of fire break, but there seems to have been no danger of the fire spreading. Apart from smoke damage to frescos and paintings, the churches were in no real danger.'

'You said this would be worth two thousand ducats each, and would take at most two months. How do you know it won't take longer?' Anthony asked.

'I don't, but it can't be allowed to take very long. We have to find answers. So far we have been able to keep it quiet, but if the murders continue, then there will be widespread panic.'

'What do you think, Hugh?' Anthony asked, turning to him.

'There's nothing I'm doing just now, and the money I certainly need.'

'Yes, I could do with the money, too. You should show

us the churches where these murders have taken place, cardinal. I can't promise anything, of course, and I don't want my wife to worry. I'm sure Hugh and I can look after ourselves, but let's keep the word murder out of it.'

'Of course. Shall we make it several thefts, involving picked locks and ciphered documents in Arabic and Gaelic. That would explain why you make the perfect team.'

'I don't know any details, indeed. Pope Clement related my entire confession to you, didn't he?'

'He was near death and he seemed unable to take your secrets to his grave. We need your skills, Sir Anthony, and yours, my lord. Anyone who can lead a rebel army and defeat the English can help track down a murderer. Will you help us?'

Cardinal Aldobrandini looked from Hugh to Anthony and back again.

'There we go now,' Hugh responded. 'So there is little left for me to lose, but Anthony, your young family is with you, whereas mine are grown.'

'Yes, but we are getting through my fortune quite quickly, and now it seems we have a sixth mouth to feed on the way.'

'Congratulations, Sir Anthony, I didn't know!' Cardinal Aldobrandini said, smiling.

'I could use the money to expand our wine production. Oh, that's a problem! We've only just started picking this year's grapes. We still have the pressing to do, and getting the fermentation off to the right start. No, it's quite impossible. I'm sorry, cardinal, I can't leave now. Perhaps at the end of September?'

'Antonio and Maria will complete the harvest. That'll work, so it will? They have good heads on themselves,' Hugh suggested.

'No.' Anthony sighed, stroking his beard, 'They are as you say, but getting the fermentation right, with the correct addition of sulphur to prevent the wine going sour, it is a delicate business.'

'Priests are dying, Sir Anthony,' Cardinal Aldobrandini whispered, leaning towards him. He swirled the wine around his goblet again and took another sip. 'When we get to Rome, I will send back our top winemaker to assist and guide Antonio and Maria. You will have the best wine you could imagine. What do you say?'

'Very well. I must show you what we've done with the vineyard before we set off.'

'Set off where?' Francesca asked, as she returned from the kitchen carrying a platter of roast lamb, followed by the twins, carrying the vegetables. Anthony fixed his eyes on Cardinal Aldobrandini. The Cardinal stood up.

'Signora Standen, there have been some mysterious thefts of valuable artworks from a few of our churches. We need to make enquiries amongst some of the more obscure art dealers, those who may export these treasures. Sir Anthony's impressive abilities in languages will be precious to us. We will reward him handsomely for his time, two thousand ducats for two months' service.'

'I see. Can you assure me it will not be dangerous?'

'Absolutely. I will accompany Anthony and Hugh with an escort from the papal guard.'

'You've already agreed to go, haven't you, Anthony?'

Francesca said, a slight tremor in her voice.

'With the money, we'll be able to expand our wine production. We are running out of money rather quickly. It's taken more than we expected to get the villa to this condition. You know we need to save a dowry for Maria, you've told me often enough.'

'Leave me out of this. I'm not for sale,' Maria said.

'Can I come with you, Father?' Antonio asked. 'It sounds interesting.'

'No, Son. I need you and Maria to look after your mother and baby brother, as well as the vineyard. There's still a lot to do here. Now can we please all just enjoy this wonderful looking feast? Fetch another flagon of our wine, please, Antonio. I'd like the cardinal's opinion. We rather like it, but he has tasted the finest wines that Rome can buy.'

Anthony was awake before sunrise. Francesca was asleep, breathing softly. He crept around the bedroom, feeling through the drawers for his clothes. He pulled on a white cotton shirt and close-fitting linen braies. Over the braies, he pulled up his tailored red-canvas breeches, and buttoned them up. He wanted something hard wearing, as he was going to be in the saddle for many weeks. He took his sheath knife and put it on his leather belt, as he threaded it through the loops in his breeches. He pulled his red-canvas smock over his shirt. Finally, he decided on his yellow silk stockings to add a touch of colour, and pulled his brown leather boots over them. He crept downstairs and noticed that the front door was open. The cardinal's fine, red-silk coat was missing from the peg in the hallway. Anthony went outside. The sun broke free of the Alban Hills and framed Cardinal Aldobrandini against the jagged outline of the new cathedral, growing from the city of Frascati, in the valley between Anthony's villa and Rome, some dozen miles to the northwest.

'I am very impressed, Sir Anthony. The villa was rather run down when the church sold it to you.'

'Yes, it took an immense amount of work to get to this point. Thankfully, the vines were in good condition, and the oak barrels needed only a little attention. I would like to buy a still, so that we can make brandy. I'd also like to plant some new vines, the Sangiovese grape, amongst the trees in the orchard yonder. I'll saddle the horses.' Anthony sighed and walked towards the stable, his eyes cast to the ground. Cardinal Aldobrandini followed, but turned as footsteps approached. Maria was carrying a bucket of leftovers from last night's meal.

'Good morning, cardinal.' Maria waved as she opened the gate to the chicken coup. Antonio followed her and headed towards the stable without glancing towards the cardinal.

'Do you have to go, Father?'

'I think so, Son. I want to make the vineyard a great success, something that you can take over; and make a good living from. You'd like that, wouldn't you?'

'Yes, but I'm not sure. I'd rather come with you and help solve the mystery of these art thefts. It sounds rather interesting.'

'I'm afraid you can't. I need you to look after your mother and the vineyard.'

'I thought the cardinal said he would send a master

winemaker to do that.'

'Maybe, but he doesn't know how we do things; and I can't trust him to look after your mother. Here, help me with the cardinal's horse, would you?' Antonio walked to the furthest stall and returned with the cardinal's bay mare. As he lifted the saddle, the stable door opened and Hugh walked in.

'Good morning, Hugh, are you ready to go?'

'That I am. Some of your cold lamb I've eaten; that doesn't bother you, I hope.'

'Of course not. Was Francesca up?'

'Sorry, she isn't to be seen just yet.'

'I hoped she would see us off. Give me a few minutes, would you?'

Anthony left the stable and walked back to the house. There was no sign of Francesca downstairs, so he went upstairs and opened their bedroom door. Francesca was standing at the window looking through a vase of flowers on the window sill, across the courtyard.

'I hoped you would come down to see us off.'

'This will be the third time you've left me. The last time you promised you'd return in a couple of months; and you were gone for nine hundred and eighty-six days. Can you promise me you will return this time?' Anthony wanted to reply, but felt the shadow of himself kneeling on the floor of his cell in the Tower of London; praying for the executioner's axe.

'You know we need the money, you agreed—' Anthony ducked as the vase of flowers smashed against the door behind him.

'I need you, not gold, or silver, or scraps of paper.'

Anthony dashed across to the window and wrapped his arms around her. He pulled her close to him. Her heart was pounding against his own, but they were out of time. He bent to kiss her, and as she turned her lips away, he kissed her cheek, tasting the salt of her tears as they cascaded down her face. Her whole body shuddered as she sobbed.

'I will come back. We will have the Swiss Guard with us. We'll be perfectly safe, I'm sure of it.' He kissed her, but she turned her face away. He kissed the nape of her neck. Francesca dropped onto their bed, curled into a ball and rolled over, away from him, her arms wrapped around her knees. Anthony closed the door behind him softly as he left.

They rode through the quiet streets of Frascati and out on the road towards Rome. Cardinal Aldobrandini rode ahead, and Hugh rode beside Anthony, a few paces behind.

'So what exactly are these special skills you have on you, Anthony?'

'It's a long story.'

'So time doesn't seem to be in short supply, so it doesn't; and not a word you have said since we left the villa.'

'I served Lord Darnley and Queen Mary in Scotland. When that came to an abrupt end, I was given a letter of introduction to the English ambassador in Paris, Sir Henry Norris. He latched onto my language skills and set me to work spying on members of the Scottish court visiting Paris. I discovered Mary's ambassador visiting the Spanish ambassador, and I tried to bribe the secretary of the Spanish ambassador to copy the relevant correspondence for me. The Spanish found out, and I was beaten to a pulp. I spent several months in a monastery recovering.'

'You don't seem to have great skills on you, just yet.'

'Do you want to hear this story or not?'

'Continue, so you should.'

'Norris thought I could be useful, so he put me with a few experts he knew. The first was his secretary, who taught me all about ciphers and codes. Then I spent several weeks with an ex-thief, who had been the son of a locksmith. From him, I became an expert in picking locks and learnt how to follow people without being observed. Finally, I learnt about wrestling from an old soldier. Shortly after, that Francis Walsingham replaced Sir Henry, and I started spying for him.'

'So when into my army you tried to enlist, the English to fight, it was me to spy on, so it was.'

'Yes, I'm sorry, Hugh. I was actually rather relieved that you didn't trust me. After Walsingham died, I became attached to the Earl of Essex. He was a great man, but rather lost his way on the campaign in Ireland. I really didn't want to spy on you, but I owed Essex a great deal.'

'My suspicion wasn't on you, you know, it was the risk I couldn't bear about me. What was it that you owed to Essex now?'

'I finally made the fortune I craved when we raided Cadiz. I'd made and lost a few fortunes in the meantime, but nothing as big as that.'

'So here you came and met the beautiful Francesca, so

you did. She does have a radiance on her.'

'Well, there were a few more twists and turns of fate in between, which I won't bore you with. We'd fallen in love many years before. Maria and Antonio were fifteen when I first met them. I had to leave then again, just for a few weeks, but it turned out to be several years.'

'What was it possessed herself to let you come this time?'

'She didn't. I must be out of my mind. I seem compelled to make more money. Perhaps it's having made and lost so many fortunes, that has made me insecure. Do you think that might be it, Hugh?'

'That'll be it, so it will. With Francesca safe and sound you'll be, I'll make it so myself, so I will, after this is done.'

They entered Rome mid-morning and made their way towards the Quirinal Palace, residence of popes since 1583. As they approached a side street, Anthony heard groans. Two women, dressed in rags, rose unsteadily from where they had been sitting, leaning against a wall. One of them held out a wooden plate. The other stayed in her shadow.

'Alms for the sick please, sir.' The fingers of her hand were black. She wore a dirty cloak with a hood. Her lips were black, and Anthony could see pustules on her neck.

'Leave them, Sir Anthony. You can do nothing for them. It is the black death, don't you see?' Cardinal Aldobrandini called back.

'Yes, I see it.' Anthony reached into his pocket and pulled out his purse. He took some small change and threw it towards the outstretched plate. Then he rode on to catch the others. When they reached the palace, a groom met them and cared for their horses, while Cardinal Aldobrandini led Hugh and Anthony to a reception room. He instructed an attendant to bring food and wine for them while he hurried off to make arrangements. Twenty minutes later, he re-joined them, accompanied by two men of the Swiss Guard, resplendent in their red-and-yellow-striped uniforms, and blue hose. An older man in a green frock-coat followed them.

'Sir Anthony, can I first introduce Signor Fratteli, a senior vintner who I will send back to assist with your harvest, and winemaking.' The man in the green frock-coat stepped forward and bowed to Anthony. He was almost a foot shorter than Anthony, but compensated for that in his circumference. Anthony wondered if his assistance with the wine production would cover the impact on their larder. As he straightened, Anthony shook his hand. His hands were the size of dinner plates.

'I am grateful for your help, Signor Fratelli. My son and daughter are able and intelligent, but we only began winemaking last year. Your guidance will be a great comfort to me.'

'And these fine men will ensure our security.' Sergeant Hennard and Guardsman Pfyffer stepped forward, shouldered their weapons, and saluted. Hennard was a little shorter than Anthony, but had broader shoulders and a square jaw. Pfyffer was taller than Hennard, but slim.

'Glad we are to have you with us,' Hugh said.

'We certainly are. Please stand easy,' Anthony added.

'I see you have flintlocks. Are they muskets or rifles?'

'Rifles, sir,' Sergeant Hennard answered.'

'Excellent, far more accurate that a musket.'

'Guardsman Pfyffer is the guard's finest marksman, sir. He can shoot a rat dead at —'

'Well, if you are both rested, can I suggest we get going. The site of the most recent atrocity is Ferrara, which is a ten-day ride from here,' Cardinal Aldobrandini said.

They left Rome, heading north. Sergeant Hennard rode alongside Cardinal Aldobrandini at the front. Hugh and Anthony rode side by side behind them and Guardsman Pyffer brought up the rear.

'You must think me terribly rude, Hugh. When you arrived at the villa, I was so keen to show you around and introduce you to my family, but I haven't asked about you. You said last night that your family is grown. Where are they?'

'In Brussels they are, my wife Catherine with our daughters, Alice and Mary, and our sons, John and Brian. The children of my previous three wives, seen I haven't in many years.'

'What are they doing in Brussels?'

'As you said yourself this morning, a long story it is, to be sure. After Essex was defeated, doing quite well I was. Then a pincer movement caught myself between Sir Charles Blount and Sir Henry Docwra, so it did. Retreat to Armagh it was that I had to do. In October 1601, the Spanish finally landed themselves an army in Kinsale, so O'Donnell and I brang our armies south to join themselves. Unfortunately, the Battle of Kinsale, a disaster for us it was. Overwhelmed we were, by a surprise English cavalry charge. Lay low I did, but like yourself, when I heard Queen Elizabeth had death upon her, to King James, I presented myself. Very gracious he was. But no sooner back to Ireland I got, than that weasel Chichester some legal precedent dug up he had, by which most of my lands to my tenants he'd given. Invited I was to visit King James again, but tipped off I was, that my arrest was imminent. Fled I did with O'Donnel and our families, and close allies, for Spain. The winds drove us east and shelter in the Seine we took. Then overland to the Spanish Netherlands we headed. Some kind of treachery was on us, I thought, because there they wanted to keep us, rather than help us get to Spain. The Spanish think I'm still in the Netherlands. So an audience with the pope himself I sought. It was his support to raise a larger Spanish army, and take back Ireland I was after now, so I was. Now don't get the anger on yourself now, but I wasn't entirely honest with yourself before, so I wasn't. I found the pope extremely troubled by these murders, and my visiting you and helping to persuade you to come on this mission, that was a precondition of his support, so it was. I would say I'm sorry to have deceived you, but you weren't entirely honest with me in, back in ninety-nine, were you now?'

Cardinal Aldobrandini was anxious to reach Ferrara as soon as possible; and the ride grew more tiring by the hour. Anthony had dropped back to ride alongside Guardsman Pfyffer. The steady tread of the horses lulled Anthony into a day dream. He thought about Francesca and their unborn child. He could see her cradling her womb. He peered closer and her fingers turned black in front of his eyes. Oozing pustules appeared on her elbows and wrists. He shook himself out of his nightmare.

'We're going to be in this for quite a while and I can't keep calling you Guardsman Pfyffer. What's your name?'

'Matteo, Sir Anthony.'

'You can drop the sir. I used to be quite precious about it, but not now. Where in Switzerland are you from?'

'Geneva. Have you been there?'

'No, but I travelled to Constantinople many years ago, with a merchant who had been to Geneva. It's close to the French border, I believe.'

'That's right. It's at the southern end of Lake Geneva; it's so very beautiful. I feel quite homesick talking about it. You don't appreciate things when you're young, do you? I wanted to see the world and have adventures, so here I am.'

'What's Sergeant Hennard's christian name?'

'I don't know, he's just sergeant to us guardsmen. He's a hard man, but fair.'

'Are you married, Matteo?'

'No, it's a requirement that you're single, to join the Swiss Guard. Are you married, Anthony?'

'Yes.'

'I see the earl is riding with the cardinal now.'

'So he is.'

'We were told our mission was to keep you safe, whilst you track down the killer of two priests. How are you going to find the killer? Should we be on the lookout for any particular type of fellow?'

'I'm afraid I have absolutely no idea. I can only hope there will be some clues when we get to Ferrara. From what I've been told, the killer burns the priests on bails of straw, soaked in brandy, and piles earth around the victim to form some sort of fire break. So if we pass anyone on a cart with bails of straw, a keg of brandy and a mound of earth, we should probably investigate.'

Matteo smiled. 'I'll keep my eyes open.'

The sun was dropping over the horizon as they entered the small town of Fiano Romano. They rode through a stone gateway and past a fortress with a tall-cylindrical tower. The cardinal had taken station beside Sergeant Hennard, at the head of their small column, and led them to a church. The cardinal dismounted and knocked on the door of a building next to the church. A priest, who bowed deeply to him, opened it. Anthony couldn't hear what was said, but the cardinal walked back to them.

'We will stay here this evening. Sergeant, you and Guardsman Pfyffer will keep watch alternately. Father Morelli will arrange supper for us, and beds for the night. Tie the horses to this rail, and he will arrange for them to be stabled, fed and watered.'

Anthony held back at dinner until Hugh had taken a seat, and then selected a seat at the far end of the table. There wasn't much conversation at dinner. Everyone seemed very tired, and perhaps apprehensive. When they retired to the dormitory, Anthony again selected a bunk as far from Hugh as he could.

As they rode north out of Fiano Romano, they passed through some ramshackle buildings outside the town's walls. There were plague victims here too. Anthony's thoughts turned again to Francesca and the baby she was bearing. He could envisage her lips turning black, and pustules forming at her joints. Why had he let himself be talked into leaving? He should be there with his wife and children. To hell with the money. Why hadn't he listened to her? Why had he let himself be led away by Hugh, who only had his own interests at heart? He'd been weak and stupid. Something burst inside him. He spurred his horse forward, drew alongside Hugh, slipped his feet from the stirrups, reached over and grabbed the reins of Hugh's horse.

'Dismount, you paddy son of a bitch!' Anthony said quietly and coldly. Hugh dismounted and drew his knife.

'No English bastard calls me that now.' Hugh and Anthony circled. Hugh lunged at Anthony. Anthony dodged the lunge and caught Hugh off balance, his hand gripping Hugh's right wrist. He threw him to the ground and quickly dropped on top of him, pinning him down. His left hand was still gripping Hugh's right wrist and whilst Hugh struggled to free himself, Anthony applied an arm lock, increasing the pressure until he could see the pain in Hugh's face.

'Drop the knife!' Hugh did drop the knife, just before Sergeant Hennard and Guardsman Pfyffer dragged Anthony off him. Hugh struggled to his feet and picked up the knife. Sergeant Hennard let go of Anthony and drew his sword. He pointed the tip at Hugh.

'Not a step nearer, sir,' Hennard ordered. Anthony started to break free from Matteo's hold, but Cardinal Aldobrandini rode up and positioned his horse between

Anthony and Hugh.

'What is this all about?'

'He deceived me, he tricked me into coming on this mission,' Anthony said, panting.

'That's not entirely true, Sir Anthony. His Holiness and I used his connection with you to help persuade you to come. We sincerely believed that together you are the best pair of minds we can use to outwit this killer. Now, if you will not work together, the sum of your brains becomes weaker than the best. I consider yours the best. So if you will not patch up your differences, then I will send Hugh back to Rome alone. Is that what you want?'

'Do what you like with the peat-munching son of a whore. I don't care,' Anthony spat, as Hugh pressed forward, until the tip of Sergeant Hennard's sword pierced his coat and dug into his skin.

'Earl O'Neill really had no choice, you know. He is only striving to secure the future of his family and return to his lands. But as you wish it, I shall send him back and advise His Holiness to waste no more effort on his behalf.'

'No, Your Eminence, I'm sorry, it's just that my wife didn't want me to leave. We didn't part on good terms, and when Hugh told me of the part he played, I suppose I blamed him.'

'Very well, I shall expect you to have made friends again by the time we reach Orte.'

'We will, Your Eminence. I'm sorry, Hugh, I didn't mean those things. I blamed you because Francesca and I didn't part on good terms. Will you forgive me?'

Hugh nodded. 'There we go now. That's fine, so it is.

Anthony, deceive yourself I did in another way as well.'

'In what way?'

'When at your villa I arrived, you asked me, so you did, if any Irish whiskey I had left. I said it was all in me. But whiskey I do have left, so I do.' He walked over to his horse and reached into his saddle bag, pulled out a flask, and passed it to Anthony.

They reached Bologna a week after leaving Anthony's villa. There was a light drizzle falling as they rode through the streets. Anthony admired the porticoed pavements which provided shelter to the pedestrians from the rain. He cricked his neck, gazing up at the immense towers as they passed. They stopped in a square, and as Cardinal Aldobrandini dismounted, they all did the same. A monk wearing a black cloak over a white habit walked briskly over to them from the large church dominating the plaza.

'Your Eminence, I saw you approaching and informed Father Abbot. If it pleases you, I will take your horses. Father Abbot will be expecting you in the abbot's house; you know the way I believe.'

'Thank you, yes.' The monk took the reins of the cardinal's horse as half a dozen other monks came to take the others. They led the horses away, and Cardinal Aldobrandini led Anthony, Hugh, and the two guardsmen to the church door. He led them down the aisle and then out of a side door. Pointing, Cardinal Aldobrandini said, 'That building is the house for higher-ranking guests. We shall stay there tonight. That includes you, sergeant and Guardsman Pfyffer. We cannot rule out an attack, even within the monastery.' They continued past another building, which the cardinal said was a school. As they approached the next building, the door opened and a tall, portly man appeared.

'Your Eminence, what an honour it is to greet you again. It must be three years, I think. Welcome to San Domenico. Welcome to your distinguished companions as well.'

'Thank you. Yes, Father Abbot Fontana, I think it was to mark Saint Dominic's day, three years ago, that I last visited.' The cardinal introduced the party, and the abbot led them into the reception room of the abbot's house. 'Sir Anthony and Earl Hugh are assisting us in a very delicate and secret matter. Sergeant Hennard and Guardsman Pfyffer are here for our protection. I am afraid that I cannot take even yourself into our confidence. We would be most grateful for some refreshment and accommodation for the night.'

'But of course. I assume from your names, Sir Anthony and Earl Hugh, that you are English?'

'I am English,' Anthony replied.

'Irish I am myself.'

'And have you been to Bologna before?'

'No,' Anthony said.

'That I haven't,' Hugh added.

'How wonderful. Then we must give you a tour of the city. The university is the oldest in Europe, you know. It was founded in 1088, some years before your Oxford. Perhaps we can do that in the morning? I'm sure you would—'

'I am afraid we must decline your generous offer,

Father Abbot. As I said, our mission is of the utmost importance. We shall leave just before dawn, and if we could dine here, in your house, rather than the refectory, that would be appreciated. The fewer who speculate on our mission, the better.'

'Of course, Your Eminence, but what a pity. I shall make the necessary arrangements. We shall provide, instead, a culinary tour of Bologna at my table, for these honoured guests. You have had a long journey. If you wish, the bathhouse is just a few doors away. I can provide clean habits for you and have your clothes laundered while we dine.'

'That would be very kind.'

An hour later, they were sitting in clean white habits around the dining table of Abbot Fontana, drinking a white wine apéritif.

'This wine is very pleasant, Father Abbot. Is it a Prosecho Tondo?' Anthony enquired.

'You know your grapes, Sir Anthony. Yes, a traditional wine that was very popular in Roman times, and still a favourite today. I am planning to serve several Sangiovese vintages, to accompany the crostini and mortadella mousse, followed by the tortellini with ragù sauce. Then we shall return to another Prosecho to wash down the guinea fowl with lemon and chopped hazelnuts. We shall cleanse our palates with a chicory salad before the cherry tart with cream. I am afraid that, as I wasn't expecting guests, we are poorly prepared, or we would have laid on a grand feast.'

'It sounds quite satisfactory, Abbot Fontana,' replied Cardinal Aldobrandini. Anthony wondered what a feast might be like, if this was everyday fare.

They set off in the early morning twilight, and with three short stops to water the horses, arrived in Ferrera in the early afternoon. The city was heavily fortified, with the river Po on its southern boundary and a wide moat running from it, completely encircling the city, before joining the river again. Immediately inside the moat was an imposing city wall. They rode across a bridge to the city gate, where the cardinal showed the guard his letter of authority and they then continued through the city. They stopped, dismounted, and tied up their horses outside the church of Santa Maria in Vado. There were guards stationed at the entrance. The guards recognised the cardinal and stepped aside to allow the party into the church.

'Gentlemen, this is the site of the second murder. If the guards have done their job, it is as it was discovered.' Cardinal Aldobrandini led them towards the altar, in front of which lay a charred skeleton. There were some fragments of straw scattered around on the stone floor. 'As you see, there is earth piled around the site of the burning. Are you alright, Sir Anthony?' Anthony was clutching his sides and shivering violently.

'Here, a drop of this'll do you good,' suggested Hugh, passing the flask with the remains of his Irish whiskey. Anthony took it with both hands and, trembling, raised the flask to his lips.

'Thank you, Hugh. I just need a minute.'

'Are you unwell, Sir Anthony?'

'No, Your Eminence. Unfortunately, when I was just a

child, during Queen Mary's reign, I witnessed the burning, in Smithfield, of the Islington martyrs, or heretics, I should say. The smells and the screams have stayed with me.'

'I see.' They stood silently for a few minutes until the whiskey took effect. 'If you are recovered, Sir Anthony, you may see here that the back of Father Caprona's skull has suffered a blow. And here is a fragment of rope.'

'Yes, it looks as though, as you said, he was knocked unconscious and then tied somehow, and set ablaze on top of the straw bales,' Anthony said as he circled around the skeleton. 'There wouldn't be any marks on the stone floor to indicate it, but I imagine he must have been knocked out somewhere else and dragged here.'

'Why do you think that?' Cardinal Aldobrandini asked.

'Well, the murderer would want to bring the straw bales in when all was quiet, in the middle of the night, perhaps. I can't imagine him hanging around and waiting for Father Caprona to turn up. I think he would have seized his victim earlier, perhaps tied and gagged him, and locked him up somewhere. He would have prepared the place of execution and then brought him here in the middle of the night.'

'A strong brute he must be.' Hugh remarked, looking at the skeleton. 'Father Caprona looks like a big man he was.'

'Yes, or he forced him to walk here with a gun or knife in his back. Perhaps he had an accomplice. When was the murder discovered?'

'On the morning after the feast day of Saint Eusebius

of Vercelli.'

'Let me see, the second of August,' Anthony said stroking his beard.

'That is the feast day, he was discovered the morning after, on the third. His deacon found him. We should talk to him later.'

'And where was the first murder?'

'In Monselice, a day's ride north from here, on the road to Padua.'

'When was that murder discovered?'

'The morning after the feast day of Saint Benedict. Oh my lord, I hadn't made that connection. Is this the work of Satan himself, murdering priests by burning, on holy days.' Cardinal Aldobrandini crossed himself.

'I don't think satan would need rope, straw and a blunt instrument. This is the work of a man, or men. Saint Benedict's Day, that's the eleventh of July, isn't it?' Anthony asked.

'Yes, yes,' Cardinal Aldobrandini stammered. The church door creaked, and they all looked round. Guardsman Pfyffer who was guarding the door levelled his musket at a short, thin young man who appeared in the doorway.

'The deacon would like to speak with you your eminence,' Guardsman Pfyffer shouted. Cardinal Aldobrandini beckoned him, and Guardsman Pfyffer smartly stood at ease. The deacon approached.

'I do beg your pardon, Your Eminence, but I wonder when we might give Father Caprona a Christian burial? And what should I say has happened. I'm constantly asked by our parishioners, and I can't explain.'

'Yes of course. Anthony, Hugh, do you see any reason not to bury what's left of Father Caprona now?'

'I do not, I think we've seen enough,' Anthony answered and Hugh nodded.

'Yes you may give Father Caprona a Christian burial. I'm afraid you must lie about the circumstances. Say that he dropped dead of unknown causes,' Cardinal Aldobrandini instructed.

'Just one thing, Deacon, sorry, what is your name?' Anthony asked.

'Nicolo, sir.'

'Well, Nicolo, you found this on the morning after the feast of Saint Eusebius I believe.'

'That's right, sir, just after sunrise. I came over to make sure the church was clean and tidy, and I found him like this.'

'Was the church door locked or unlocked?'

'Locked, sir. That was the worrying thing. When I saw what had happened, I picked up a candlestick and went around to check all the doors. They were all locked, sir. Do you think the killer was hiding and slipped out after I had opened the door? I didn't hear any footsteps.'

'Perhaps, but I doubt it.'

'How many keys are there, Nicolo?' the cardinal asked.

'Only two, Your Eminence. I have one, and Father Caprona has one, had one Your Eminence.'

'Has his key been found?'

'No, Your Eminence.'

'What do you make of this, Anthony?'

'The killer may have been lying in wait, and when the

priest opened the door, he knocked him out, took his key, and dragged him inside. Then he rushed back out to his cart and dragged the bales of straw in, possibly with the aid of an accomplice. But it seems a bit risky. It would have been safer to make all the preparations in the middle of the night.'

'But how could he have done that without a key?' asked the cardinal.

'I'll show you.' Anthony walked over to the door and everyone followed him. He opened the door and then closed it again. He locked the door with the key, and then withdrew the key and gave it to Sergeant Hennard. Then he took a small leather case from a pocket in his doublet and extracted two metal rods with hooked ends. Anthony knelt down and inserted the rods in the keyhole. He twisted each in turn for almost a minute, then stood up and opened the door. 'It takes a few weeks to learn the art of lock picking, and months to perfect it, but with constant practice, it's quite simple.'

'Good lord. Are there many people who can do this?'

'All good locksmiths, myself, and some criminals. Nicolo, we have heard you smelled brandy on the morning you found Father Caprona. Is that right?'

'Yes, sir. The smell was quite distinctive. I picked up some of the unburnt straw, and the smell was strong on it. There is something else, sir. I found the door of the presbytery open, and there are some blood stains on the floor, or at least they look like blood.'

'Would you mind showing us?' Anthony asked. Nicolo led them all to the presbytery next door where Father Caprona had lived. Nicolo took out a key and opened the door. He pointed to a dried red stain on the stone threshold. Anthony bent down, licked his finger and touched the stain. He put his finger to his nose, then touched his tongue. 'It's blood all right.' Anthony said as he went further inside. The house was sparsely furnished. There was a writing desk with paper and quill. There was a candlestick on the desk with a burnt-out stub in it. He looked at the paper. 'A half-finished sermon, by the look of it. For my money, he was interrupted by a knock on the door. He opened it and was whacked over the head, possibly after a brief struggle. He may have been bound here and then taken to the church.'

'Is there anything else you want to look at here, Sir Anthony, Earl Hugh?' the cardinal asked.

'Thank you. I think perhaps we should be off to Monselice now, Your Eminence. I would like to see if it is exactly the same.'

'Yes, Anthony. Take Hugh and Guardsman Pfyffer with you. I will catch you up with Sergeant Hennard. I must see the bishop here and make arrangements for Father Caprona's funeral, and also for services to be reinstated for the good people of this parish.'

CHAPTER THREE

Hugh and Anthony rode side by side out of Ferrara, and onto the road to Monselice. Guardsman Pfyffer followed them.

'So what do you make of it, Hugh? Why would anyone burn a priest like that?'

'He would have the revenge on him now.'

'What could these two priests have done to him, that could make him do this?'

'That I don't know, and that firebreak. What is that about? To be sure, there was no danger of the fire spreading laterally, and the ceiling was very high, so it was. There was no chance of it setting the roof ablaze. Anyway, if it was the two priests that this fellow hated so much, he was hardly likely to worry about setting a church alight, now, was he? Symbolic it is, in some way, I think? Fire and dirt, heat and soil? It's puzzled I am.'

'A symbol, a statement. I think you may have something there, Hugh. There's something nagging at the back of my mind, but I can't work out what it is. It's something someone said.'

'In the last few days, was it?'

'No, I don't think so.'

'Well, stop thinking about it and just ride. Then it'll be about you in no time. The murderer must have passed along this road you realise, sometime in July, in his cart with his straw and brandy about him. I wonder where it is he is now? Hey Matteo, if you see any men with a cart-load of straw, then search them we should. If a keg of brandy and those little rods like Anthony's they have on them, then that'll be them, so it will.'

'Yes, sir.'

By late afternoon, it became clear that they couldn't reach Monselice before sunset; so they found an inn in Rovigo and took rooms for the night. They were all tired, so took a simple meal, and some wine, and retired for the night. The following morning, they set off early and reached their destination before noon.

'Do we know which church it is that we're looking for, Anthony?' Hugh called out.

'I suggest we ride around until we find one that's boarded up, or has a guard outside.'

The town was in a valley overlooked by a castle on a hill. They rode through the streets and pulled up in front of a church with a notice pinned to its door which read "Vietato l'ingresso"

'This is it,' said Anthony as he dismounted. 'Santa Giustina.' He tried the door, but it was locked. He got out his lock picks and started working on the lock.

'Hey there, what are you doing?' They all turned around to see a short hunchback in clerical robes limping towards them. 'Nobody is allowed in there until Cardinal Aldobrandini's men arrive.'

'We are Cardinal Aldobrandini's men,' said Guardsman Pfyffer. 'Don't you recognise the uniform of the Swiss Guard?'

'Yes, but who are these other men?'

'They are investigators appointed by Pope Paul. Do you want to delay Pope Paul's investigation and wait for the cardinal, he should be here in a few hours, but I don't think he will appreciate the delay.'

'Very well, I have the key,' the hunchback said, pushing Anthony away from the door.

'I'd better go in first,' Guardsman Pfyffer said. Hugh and Anthony stood aside. 'All clear,' he said. 'It looks just like the last one.'

Anthony and Hugh approached the charred skeleton, looking for any signs of a struggle, but there were none. A silver crucifix, distorted from the heat, with embedded rubies, still hung around his neck. Once again there were pieces of straw scattered about, and a circular earth bund about a foot tall surrounded the skeleton. They left Matteo to keep watch while they explored the rest of the church. The hunchback followed closely behind them. Anthony left Hugh to examine the scene and turned to the hunchback.

'What was his name?'

'Father Valenti,' the hunchback replied. 'I knew it was Father Valenti from his crucifix. As you see, it is quite ornate. He was very proud of it.'

'I'm sorry, I should have asked your name. Who are you?'

'I'm his deacon, Cesare Pelisi.'

'You don't seem to be particularly upset. Why is that?'

'Father Valenti had an unhealthy appetite for choirboys. He very slowly drew them into his web. He made them fear him and did abominable things to them. No, I'm not sorry he's dead.'

'My god! Why didn't you report him to the bishop?'

'Hah! Report him to the bishop! Bishop Martino was the priest here when I was a choirboy. I was not a pretty boy, as you can imagine. He had no appetite for me, but he did have an appetite for one or two of the others. Marco was a friend of mine. He told his father what had happened, but his father was a drunken brute and beat him for telling lies. The next day, they found that Marco had hung himself from a beam in their stable. His father drank himself to death and his mother died of heartbreak. Tell Bishop Martino indeed. I fear that man more than satan himself.'

'So the same thing it is, Anthony,' Hugh said as he re-joined Anthony and Deacon Pelisi.

'It's so cold in here. Let's get out into the sunshine,' Anthony suggested. Hugh and Matteo followed him outside. Deacon Pelisi remained in the church. 'There's an inn over there. Let's get a drink and some bread and cheese.' They were soon seated and enjoying some beer and a light lunch. Anthony felt the heat of the sun on his face. He put down his tankard.

'I had a talk with the hunchback. Father Valenti abused choirboys. He couldn't tell the bishop, because he's just as bad.'

'It's not so common, but it's not so rare either. It

happens in Ireland too.'

'It provides a motive. Do you think the deacon could have done it?'

'Himself you mean? Lift bales of straw? Doubt it I do.'

'Well, it could be another ex-choirboy, or one of their fathers, perhaps.'

'If it was myself that had the motive,' Hugh said, rolling the words around his mouth. 'Whack him I would over the head, and bind his wrists and ankles. There we go now. Gag him too, I would. Then his balls I'd cut off. Maybe his cock, too. I might hope that bleed to death he didn't, but live with the consequences about himself. Muck about with bales of straw and brandy, it's too dangerous, that I wouldn't do. Why on earth, tell me that, why the priest in Ferrara would I slaughter, in that same strange way?'

'Good point! I think I'd do the same. You haven't said anything, Matteo?'

'I'm not paid to speak, sir.'

'Perhaps, but you have eyes and ears, and a brain. What do you make of it?'

'Well, you hear things you can hardly believe. But I agree with Earl O'Neill. Why the earth and the burning? I'd certainly cut the balls from the bastard and stuff them down his throat. I'm sorry, sir, I'm better at following orders, I think that's best.'

'I think I've remembered what it was.'

'What is it that you've remembered?' asked Hugh.

'What was bothering me about the earth. You remember, the symbology of it, fire and earth. The fire at the centre and the surrounding earth. Back in 1603, when I was delivering the news of the accession of King James to the pope, Pope Clement, that was, he offered to hear my confession. We got talking afterwards about science, because I had told him about the alchemy I had learnt when helping the Duke of Tuscany. He told me about some lunatic of a scientist who thinks that the Earth revolves around the sun. Do you see, fire representing the sun, and earth, as the Earth, placed around it.' Anthony looked expectantly at Hugh.

'So the symbolism, what does that have to do with the murder of two priests?'

'I don't know, but I think it's important.'

Anthony, Hugh and Matteo were nearing the end of their second beers when they saw Cardinal Aldobrandini and Sergeant Hennard approaching. Matteo drained his tankard, jumped up, and placed the tankard on a neighbouring table. He then took up a sentry position behind Anthony and Hugh. When the cardinal and Sergeant Hennard had dismounted and tied up their horses, they joined the others. Guardsman Pfyffer pulled two chairs from an empty table over for them.

'Have you inspected the scene of the first murder?' Cardinal Aldobrandini enquired.

'Yes, and it's exactly the same as the scene in Ferrera, but I think I've worked out the significance of the earth surrounding the victim. Fire and Earth. If the fire represents the sun, and the earth represents the Earth, then however crazy it may seem, someone is trying to suggest that the Earth revolves around the sun. Now I hope you can help me, Your Eminence, because Pope Clement told me about a scientist who thought the Earth revolved around the sun, but I can't remember his name.'

'There have been a few who have sought to argue against the holy scriptures. There was a German priest, Nicolaus Copernicus, who died before we could investigate him. He studied at the university in Bologna, incidentally. I believe you are probably thinking of Galileo Galilei. He is the professor in science and mathematics at the university in Padua. Cardinal Bellarmine has been monitoring his work. He is permitted to teach the theory of the Copernican model, but not to defend it. From what I've heard of him, he seems an unlikely murderer, although he is a tall, strong fellow.'

'I think we should interview him, Your Eminence,' Anthony said.

'Very well, we shall go to Padua. We can be there before dusk if we go now. There is a friend of Galileo that I think you should interview as well, Paolo Sarpi. He is a leading Venetian lawyer, and at the centre of a rebellion against the pope's authority. This rebellion by the Venetians has broken out at the same time as these murders. It is too much of a coincidence. It would be interesting if Sarpi were proven to be behind these murders.' They got up, untied their horses, and mounted. Anthony rode beside the cardinal.

'What is the nature of the rebellion that Sarpi is at the centre of, Your Eminence?'

'Our nuncio in Venice informed Pope Clement that Sarpi was in regular correspondence with heretics, and that he denied the immortality of the soul. Pope Paul tried to correct the cancerous heresy that seemed to be abroad in Venice, and rightly so. The Venetians then invented some, supposedly ancient laws, that forbade the building of new churches without the consent of the Venetian state. They also passed laws forbidding the acquisition of property by the church. They demanded that secular tribunals have the right to try ecclesiastics. In April last year, the pope excommunicated the Venetians as a whole. Sarpi then began publishing numerous pamphlets undermining papal authority. King Henry of France mediated a compromise in April this year, but Venice retained the right to try priests in their courts, and they made Sarpi a state counsellor.'

'I see, so you think this Sarpi might hate the church enough to have murdered two priests. Yet it sounds as though he might be quite happy with his standing in Venice at the moment, and if I were he, I would probably want to stay there.'

'Which is why he would send mercenaries to do his dirty work. Obviously, I daren't accompany you to Venice, but it would be very convenient if you did find something on Sarpi.'

'We will make a thorough investigation, Your Eminence.'

They entered the city of Padua through an enormous, and quite new-looking, monumental gate, just before dusk. Cardinal Aldobrandini led them to the heart of the city, dominated by a massive basilica.

'Sir Anthony, I thought it appropriate that we should stay with the good monks of the Basilica of Saint

Anthony. We know your namesake as the saint of miracles and lost things.'

'I think we are going to need a miracle,' Anthony murmured. They all dismounted. Cardinal Aldobrandini led the way to the main door of the monastery. Their horses were taken to the stables, and they went to meet the abbot. Once more, the cardinal explained the secrecy of their mission to the abbot and they ate in the abbot's private dining room. Father Abbot Bianchi was courteous, but left them after the main course.

'Excuse me, Your Eminence, I have a lot of work to do. May the lord be with you on your mission.'

'Thank you, Father Abbot.' When the door had closed behind the abbot, the cardinal began again. 'Tomorrow we shall talk with the chancellor of the university. I shall explain that you have the full papal authority to investigate and interrogate any member of the university, present and past, and that it will be in his best interest to assist you. I think I should leave the interrogation of Galileo to you.' He raised his hand as Anthony was about to speak. 'Although I would like to hear what he has to say, I believe he may be more open if I am not present. I shall return to Rome with Guardsman Pfyffer to ensure my safety. The greater authority and experience of Sergeant Hennard should, I think, be at your disposal. Remember, I want you to investigate Paolo Sarpi with the utmost rigour.' Cardinal Aldobrandini turned to Sergeant Hennard. 'Before you go to Venice, you will need some different clothes. The uniform of the Swiss Guard will mark you out as an enemy of their state, for the present.'

'Yes, Your Eminence,' Sergeant Hennard replied.

'Cardinal, I recall that you said some treasures from churches stolen they were. What can you tell us about those now?' Hugh enquired.

'Yes, these murders have somewhat overshadowed the thefts. There was an outbreak of thefts in May and June, right here in Padua, but there have also been reports of thefts in Venice. There were half a dozen gold candlesticks, and a jewelled gold chalice taken from the treasury of the cathedral here. In Venice we hear that several paintings by Bellini, have been taken, along with the Crucifixion by Foppa.'

'Was it on the saint's days, stolen they were?'

'Of that we aren't sure. The Venetians are unhelpful, and we only know the last date that the gold candlesticks and chalice were checked. That is why we can only say that the theft must have occurred either in May or June. They were seen on Saint Athanasius's Day, and were missing by the Nativity of Saint John the Baptist. Oh my goodness, that's the connection. There was no force used. The treasury door and the chest from which the treasures were taken, were still locked. We have been blaming the bishop for allowing the key to fall into the wrong hands, but we didn't imagine the locks could be unlocked and relocked without the key. It must be the same man.'

'Why would a very successful thief, so he is, suddenly to murder turn, and of such a peculiar nature?' Hugh asked.

'And why would the murderer begin with thefts?' Anthony added. They finished their dessert, drained their goblets, and retired to the important guest accommodation.

CHAPTER FOUR

The chancellor's office was enormous and well lit by two windows facing south. The chancellor sat behind a broad desk facing the door, with the windows behind him. He stood up as the party entered. He was of medium height and slim, with the slight stoop of a man who spends too much time behind a desk. He was wearing a black gown, with a yellow-trimmed hood hanging down at the back, over a purple doublet. He wore white silk stockings under yellow breeches, and black buckled-shoes. The east wall was covered with bookshelves. There was a fireplace on the opposite wall with a log fire blazing. Whilst Cardinal Aldobrandini was making introductions, Anthony looked at the books. They were ordered first by size, then by subject, and finally, alphabetically by author.

'Please sit down, Your Eminence, and honoured guests. How can I help you?' the chancellor asked as he walked over to a small table beside the door, and carried a chair back to his desk, placing it beside the three chairs already arranged in front of his desk. They all sat down.

'I am afraid there is very little that I can tell you about our enquiries. The subject is extremely delicate. However, Sir Anthony and Earl Hugh must be given every assistance in their investigations, and full access to the university staff, students and records. They have full papal authority for this, and you must ensure that they are given everything they ask for.'

'I see. Yes, of course I will ensure they have everything they need, Your Eminence. Do you know how long the investigations will take? Most of the staff have returned to prepare for the start of term. If you could complete your investigations before term starts in earnest on Monday, that would be very helpful.'

'Today is Wednesday. Do you think that will be enough time, Sir Anthony?'

'If we have every assistance as promised, then I hope so, Your Eminence,' Anthony replied. 'Chancellor, we would like to begin by interviewing Galileo Galilei. Is he one of the members of staff that have returned for the start of term?'

'Oh yes. He lives in the city. He has a young family, two daughters and a son, Vincenzo, born only last year. I pity him, really. His father was a musician and left him with considerable debts, which is probably why he didn't marry. But having daughters born out of wedlock will be a considerable burden on him. They will almost certainly have to go into a convent. He is always working to find the invention that will make his fortune.'

'I know how he feels,' Anthony murmured.

'Would you like me to take you to his study?' the chancellor asked.

'Please take Sir Anthony and Earl Hugh. I think Galileo will speak more freely without my presence, or indeed yours, chancellor,' Cardinal Aldobrandini replied. 'I have to return to Rome now. Sergeant Hennard, I suggest that you stand guard outside whenever there are interrogations in progress. I shall be quite safe, I think, making my way back to Rome with Guardsman Pfyffer. Don't forget to visit a tailor.'

'Yes, Your Eminence,' said Sergeant Hennard, who stood up as the cardinal rose from his seat. Anthony, Hugh, and the chancellor also stood up.

'Well, we may as well all start now,' the chancellor said, as he walked across and opened his study door. Guardsman Pfyffer stood to attention as the door opened and the cardinal strode out.

'Pfyffer, would you be so kind as to escort me back to Rome?'

'Of course, Your Eminence.'

Galileo's study was the sort of room that spiders love and cleaners don't. The bookshelves were full, leaving no space for the stacks of books dotted around the floor. Several books lay open on his desk, along with an inkwell and a pot of quills. The room was a little smaller than the chancellor's study, yet still a generous size. Even so, the chancellor led Anthony and Hugh through a zig-zag course towards Galileo, avoiding the stacks of books and small tables supporting various models, a globe, and musical instruments.

'These gentlemen are here to ask you a few questions, Galileo. They act with the authority of the pope. This is Sir Anthony Standen, and this is Hugh O'Neill, Earl of Tyrone. I shall leave you now. You know where I am if you need me.'

'Yes, yes, let me see, there are two chairs here somewhere.' As Galileo stood up, Anthony noticed that he was a good three inches taller than Hugh. Hugh was an inch taller than Anthony, who was, himself, a couple of inches taller than average. He was also broad in the chest and powerfully built. He had piercing, enquiring eyes, and a long, straggly beard. He took a lute and a pair of brass calipers from the seat of a chair, and brushed a pile of books to one side with his foot, to make room for it in front of his desk. He took a wooden model from the seat of another chair. 'This is the model for a horse-powered pump I am working on,' he explained, as he put it on top of a stack of books and placed the second chair in front of his desk. 'Please sit down. What is it you want to discuss?'

'Can you tell us where you were on the feast day of Saint Benedict?' Anthony asked. Galileo rummaged through the books on his desk and opened a notebook. He began thumbing through the pages.

'I spent the afternoon with the local blacksmith; showing him my design for a hydrostatic balance. He has since made a working model of it for me. I attended mass in the cathedral in the evening.'

'Can anyone confirm you were at the mass?'

'The chancellor and his wife were there. The bishop

would remember me too, I expect.'

'And what about on the feast day of Saint Eusebius?' Anthony asked. Galileo turned the page of his notebook.

'I was in Venice visiting the Arsenal. The model of the horse-powered pump is of a design I am working on for the manager there. Why do you ask?'

'We are investigating some crimes that took place on those days. We will check your alibis, but it would appear you have nothing to worry about.'

'Oh, I have everything to worry about. My sister's brother is suing me for the dowry that my late father promised, but couldn't pay. My youngest brother is constantly borrowing money. I have no dowry for my daughters.' Galileo shuddered as he spoke and ran his fingers through his thick hair.

'I am sorry, I know something of what you feel,' Anthony whispered. 'I'm told you believe that the sun is at the centre of the universe, rather than the earth. Is that right?'

'I don't believe it, I know it.'

'How do you know it? We see the sun rise every morning and go down at night. It is clearly orbiting around us,' Anthony said. Galileo walked over to a table and came back with a globe.

'If the earth is rotating like this, and you are the sun, then a person here,' he said, pointing to Rome on the globe, 'would see you rising and setting. Now I have a book De Revolutionibus Orbium Coelestium, written by Nicolaus Copernicus, yes here it is.' He plucked it from his bookshelves and handed it to Anthony. 'It contains diagrams and tables of the motion of the planets, based upon their rotation around the sun. I have spent many years observing the stars and the planets, and his theory describes their motions precisely. It works! I am also working on a theory of the tides.' Galileo picked up a vase of water from his window sill and discarded some wilted flowers. 'Now, if I tilt the vase, the water moves. If I blow on the water's surface, waves form. And if I rotate the vase around me, the water sloshes back and forth. We have two motions, the earth orbiting the sun once per year, and the earth spinning one revolution per day. I have shown mathematically that the sum of these movements produces the accelerations and decelerations that give us the twelve-hour tidal cycle.'

'But the moon causes the tides,' Anthony stated.

'The moon has nothing to do with it. It's all in my calculations, here,' Galileo flung a sheath of papers into Anthony's lap.' Anthony made a pretence of reading the calculations, but they were too advanced for him.

'I see, and do you teach your students that the sun is at the centre, and we orbit around it?'

'No, adamantly no. I teach my students to observe, to think, to model, to experiment, and to conclude. What they learn is up to them.'

'How many students do you have?'

'Twelve at present.'

'We need a list of your present and past students.'

'I could make one from memory, but the chancellor has a list. Could you get it from him? I really must get back to work.'

'There's just one more thing. I believe you are a friend of Paolo Sarpi. What can you tell us about him?'

'Yes, he is a friend and a patron. He is also a brilliant scientist in his own right. He was a student here, you know.'

'Does he also believe that the Earth orbits the sun?'

'Yes, of course.'

'Is he a violent man?'

'Not in the slightest. He is a priest, a canon lawyer, a scientist and a statesman. He will debate with you all night until the sun rises, but he wouldn't harm a hair on your head.'

'Do you write to him?'

'Yes, often. There are various projects that we are working on together.'

'Then you can give us his address.'

'Yes, of course.' Galileo scribbled it on a scrap of paper and handed it to Anthony. 'Is there anything else?'

'No, thank you. You have been very helpful.'

Hugh and Anthony left Galileo's study. Sergeant Hennard was waiting outside. They walked together back to the chancellor's office.

'So what is it you make of him, Anthony?' Hugh asked.

'Well, he's clearly very intelligent, but he's wrong about the moon and tides. If you've sailed in the English Channel, you can't fail to notice the change in the tides. The tidal range between high and low water reaches a maximum at new moon and full moon, and it's at a minimum for the half-moons. We can check out his alibis, then we need to check up on his students. There is a killer somewhere who has a grudge against the church, and I'm convinced it has something to do with the Earth orbiting the sun.'

The chancellor confirmed that Galileo had been at mass on the feast day of Saint Eusebius. He also asked his clerk to provide Anthony with a list of Galileo's present and former students.

'We need to know where each of these students were on the nights of the feast days of Saint Benedict and Saint Eusebius. Can you do that?'

'For the current students, we will try. For the former students, we can run checks on those who have remained in the city. For the others, we can only provide you with the addresses they have given us. You would be best contacting their parish priest and taking it from there. Will you be staying in the monastery for a few days? Can I reach you there?'

'Yes, if we're not in, leave a message.'

They left the university and went to visit the blacksmith. He confirmed that Galileo had spent the afternoon of Saint Benedict's Day with him, working on a model of a balance. Then they found an inn for lunch.

'You could ride from here to Monselice in three hours at a push, so you could. Even if he was at mass, he could have got there in the early hours of the morning to kill the priest, to be sure,' Hugh suggested.

'Not on a cart with bales of straw, a keg of brandy and a mound of earth. If he was in Venice for Saint Eusebius's day, then he definitely couldn't have reached Ferrara in less than two days. Besides, did he look like a murderer to you?'

'Well, he has the build for it, but to be honest, he did

not. So what is it we are going to do with this list of students?'

'I suggest we make a copy and send Sergeant Hennard to Rome with the original. The cardinal can seek corroboration of alibis from the parish priests whilst we go to Venice. Is that all right with you, sergeant?'

'Well, I don't know. I'm supposed to be guarding you both.'

'We can look after ourselves.'

'With the greatest of respect, Sir Anthony and Earl O'Neill, how old are you?'

'I'm fifty-eight,' Anthony replied.

'It's barely fifty-seven I am,' Hugh added.

'It's out of the question, I'm afraid. If I were to leave two elderly men that I've been instructed to guard with my life, I'd be locked up, or worse. I mean, I've seen you brawling together earlier, and had to pull you apart. But I'm thirty years younger than you, and a professional, trained soldier. It's my job to guard you.'

'Elderly, elderly, did you say? Right, come on, up you get, sergeant! We'll have a little sport. Come on, get up!' Anthony ordered, and Sergeant Hennard stared at Anthony for a few seconds. Then he drained the last drops of ale from his tankard and slowly lowered the tankard to the table. He pushed his chair back and stood up. Hugh did the same. Anthony led them round the side of the inn where they found a patch of grass. There was nobody nearby. 'Hit me, sergeant, as hard as you can!'

'I must protest, sir.'

'Just hit me!'

'Well, if you insist.' The sergeant turned to his right

and looked behind him. As he turned, he raised his right arm, the movement being hidden from Anthony's view by his body. He swung back to face Anthony, whilst his right fist arced in a neat right-hook towards Anthony's jaw. In a split second, he was lying on his back screaming, as Anthony was knelling beside him, applying an arm lock.

'Had enough, sergeant?'

'Yes! How did you do that?' He rubbed his right elbow with the palm of his left hand.

'I learnt to wrestle from a past-master, a short soldier who needed technique to compensate for his stature. He taught me a few killer moves too, which come in very handy if you're attacked by a group of men.'

'What about you, Earl O'Neill? Do you wrestle too?'

'No, it's plain dirty, I fight. Will you be wanting to try me?'

'No, I believe you.'

'As I was saying, we can look after ourselves. And the sooner we narrow down the list of suspects, the sooner we find the killer, and the sooner I get back to my wife and family,' Anthony explained.

'I suppose if you put it like that, then yes.'

'Excellent! Shall we go back to the inn and see if our lunch is ready?' Anthony suggested.

The following day, they returned to the chancellor's office.

'All the current students have alibis. We won't have the list of ex-students ready until tomorrow, at the earliest.'

'In that case, I wonder if you could make two lists.

The first list should be a complete list of the ex-students, with last known location. The second list should comprise those ex-students with addresses in Padua, or between Padua and Florence,' Anthony asked.

'Yes, we could do that.'

'Hugh and I have business to attend to in Venice. Sergeant Hennard will call in tomorrow for the first list. We will return for the second list when we get back from Venice.' They bade the chancellor farewell and returned to the monastery.

'Why the second list now, Anthony?' Hugh asked.

'It will take us three days at most to get to Venice, interview Sarpi and get back here. It will take Sergeant Hennard ten days to get back to Rome. The cardinal will then need to arrange messengers to ride out to all the addresses on the list. We can work our way through the second list, probably eight days before the first ex-student from the first list is cleared.'

'The cardinal's team will work outwards from Rome, and start at this end, working back towards Rome, we will. That makes sense,' Hugh smiled. 'So is it this morning that we leave for Venice?'

'Yes, I'm actually rather looking forward to visiting Venice. When I was recruited as a spy, my first cover story was that I was a Venetian wine merchant, and as I said, the sooner we catch this killer, the sooner I see Francesca. Lord, I hope she's forgiven me.' here.

CHAPTER FIVE

Anthony and Hugh rode into Mestre just before dusk. They made their way through the streets, found an inn in the main square, and tied up their horses. They secured rooms for the night, and the landlord agreed to stable their horses until they had completed their business in Venice. The following morning, they walked down to the quayside. They could see the walls and towers of Venice appearing to rise from the sea, a defiant Atlantis determined not to drown. There were some sailing boats at the quay. They boarded one that didn't bear the stench of a fishing boat, but looked designed for ferrying merchants back and forth across the lagoon, to the islands of Venice.

'Where are you from?' asked the helmsman as he took their fare.

'We're English,' Anthony replied. Hugh winced.

'You're Italian is perfect, signore. If you told me you

were from Rome, I wouldn't have doubted it. Have you been to Venice before?'

'No, it's my first visit.'

'Sit here, near me, and I will point out the sights. Does your friend speak Italian?'

'Yes, quite well.'

Once they had cast off, pushed off the quay and hoisted the sail, the helmsman gave a running commentary. The winds were moderate from the southwest, and it was a pleasant sail across the lagoon towards the Canale della Giudecca. The boat leant to the wind and surged forwards. Anthony and Hugh were seated on the starboard side, and Anthony could put his arm over the gunwale and feel the water rushing through his fingers. He thought about the time he had spent as a fisherman in Flanders, learning the ropes so that he could join William of Orange's navy, the Sea Beggars. He smiled as he thought about Walter and his other shipmates. His smile faded as he remembered the shipmates who had died, the men he had killed, and the atrocities he had witnessed. Once in the canal, their speed dropped a little as they crossed the wind shadows of buildings on the island of La Giudecca. As they had passed the magnificent dome of the Church del Santissimo Redentore, the helmsman turned northeast. The crewman eased the sail out, and they ran with the wind directly behind them towards an immensely tall tower.

'The tower directly ahead is the Campanile of Saint Mark. Behind it is Saint Mark's Basilica, and the big building to the right is the Palazzo Ducale.'

As they approached the quayside, the crewman went up to the bow and began shouting and waving at the boatmen already tied up at the quay. There was a flurry of activity ashore and two boats were moved apart, creating a space that didn't look quite large enough. The helmsman shouted at the crewman, who took a rope from the end of the boom and secured it to a pin on the gunwale forward of the sail. The helmsman then turned further to the east, and the boat slowed as the sail backed. The noise of the flapping sail drowned out all conversation. After less than a minute, the helmsman turned to the west. The crewman released the rope from its pin and the sail filled again. The boat surged towards the quayside. 'Giù,' shouted the helmsman, and the crewman released the mainsail halyard. The sail dropped, and the crewman took hold of a mooring rope that he had secured to the boat's side. He climbed onto the side of the boat, holding the mooring rope in one hand. and jumped onto the quay as they glided alongside it. He wrapped the rope around a bollard, and they came to a gentle halt. Anthony stood up and looked fore and aft. They were not more than a foot clear from the boats ahead and astern.

'I have done some sailing myself, captain, and I applaud you,' Anthony said.

'I sail every day, signor. Enjoy your visit!' the helmsman replied, grinning. Anthony pulled out of his purse the paper on which Galileo had written Sarpi's address.

'Can you point us in the right direction for this address, captain?'

'It's about two hundred yards east of the Palazzo

Ducale, on the waterfront.'

'Thank you again,' Anthony said as he and Hugh stepped onto the quay.

They lingered a minute, admiring the Palazzo Ducale. To its left, rose the campanile bell tower. The Basilica of Saint Mark jutted out from behind the Palazzo Ducal, and its magnificence pulled Anthony towards it; Hugh followed. As they passed the campanile, a vast square opened up to their left. There were clusters of people all across the square, and some sat outside taverns, enjoying a drink. Anthony wandered around, passing between the small assemblies.

'What is it you're doing, Anthony? I thought we were going to speak to Sarpi.'

'Yes, I'm sorry, but isn't it fascinating?'

'What is it that you mean, now?'

'The languages. I've heard Italian, Arabic, French, German, Spanish, and several languages I haven't heard before. They seem to flit effortlessly between tongues. I thought I was an excellent linguist, but these Venetians put me to shame.'

'What is it they're talking about?'

'Trade. It's all about merchandise, price, and delivery dates. You're right though, let's find Sarpi.'

They traced their steps to the quayside and turned left. They crossed a bridge over a narrow canal, and to their left they saw a beautiful enclosed, white-limestone bridge connecting the palace to a building about two thirds of the palace's height with horizontal and vertical bars across every window.

'Would that be a prison now, do you think?' Hugh asked.

'That's what it looks like,' Anthony replied, folding his arms across his chest. They continued walking along the quay, crossing another bridge over a narrow canal. They glanced at the nameplates beside each door as they passed.

'There we go now, this is it!' said Hugh. 'Fra Paolo Sarpi. Shall I knock now?'

'Go ahead. I'll do the talking. You watch him and see if you think he's telling the truth. You're better at that than I am.' Hugh used the large bronze knocker on the heavy wooden door. They could hear footsteps. The door opened and a middle-aged woman in a plain, full-length dress, with long arms and a hood, peered at them.

'We would like to speak with Brother Sarpi. We are friends of Galileo Galilei.' Anthony said.

'Wait here,' the woman said as she turned and went back down the corridor. Moments later, she returned. 'He will see you, come please.' They followed her to a door off to the right. She opened it and waved them in, closing the door behind them. A distinguished-looking man, with piercing eyes, a high forehead, and wearing the grey habit of the Servite Order, rose from the seat at his desk and came over to greet them.

'It is always a pleasure to meet friends of Galileo. I am Paolo,' he said, holding out his hand. Anthony shook it first.

'I am Sir Anthony Standen, and this is Hugh O'Neill, Earl of Tyrone.'

'An Englishman and an Irishman. What brings you to

Venice, some trading perhaps? Please sit down,' he said as he returned to his seat. Hugh and Anthony sat in the two chairs in front of the desk. 'I have friends in England, perhaps you know them?'

'There are a lot of men in England, sir, it is unlikely.'

'William Harvey, the physician, I am in regular correspondence with him about anatomy.'

'No, I haven't heard of him.'

'Then what about Francis Bacon?'

'Francis, why yes, I know him well. I was wrong. It is a small world, after all. I know his brother Anthony, much better. We worked together once. They were good friends of the Earl of Essex, Robert Devereux, God rest his soul.' Hugh remained silent. 'I lived with Anthony and Francis in Gray's Inn for many weeks, and stayed with them at their brother's second home, Twickenham Park. The Earl of Essex's country home, Barn Elms, was just across the river. I stayed there a few times too. I spent Christmas 1593 there.'

'Well, well, but you said it was Galileo who sent you. How do you know him? Are you scientists too?'

'Not exactly, although I have dabbled in alchemy. We are investigating the murders of two priests. They were killed in very curious, and most unpleasant circumstances.'

'Really, what were the circumstances, and why do they bring you here, to me?'

'They were bludgeoned over the head and tied up. Then they were set atop brandy-soaked bales of straw in their churches, and set alight at night. There was an earth mound surrounding the fire, although there was no danger of the fire spreading in either instance. It nagged me for sometime, but now I think it has something to do with heliocentricity. That is why we spoke with Galileo, and why we are speaking to you. Do you believe that the Earth orbits the sun?'

'The body of scientific proof convinces me, yes.'

'Then can you tell us where were you on Saint Benedict's Day and Saint Eusebius's Day?'

'Here in Venice. I have been working quite hard in defence of the state's freedoms. I haven't set foot outside the city since last summer.'

'Are there witnesses that can attest that you were in the city on and around Saint Benedict's Day and Saint Eusebius's Day, specifically?'

'I will check my notebook.' Paolo opened a large, leather-bound book on his desk and leafed through the pages. 'Saint Benedict's Day was Saturday, the eleventh of July. The work of the council never ends. I was in council meetings most of the day in the Palazzo Ducal. In the evening I visited the printer to approve the draft of my book Riposta di un Dottore in Teologia. You know Venice had just been excommunicated. The following morning, I attended mass in the cathedral of Saint Mark.' Paolo flicked forwards through a dozen or so pages. 'Saint Eusebius's Day was Sunday, the second of August. Why, Galileo was visiting. We both attended mass in the cathedral in the morning. We had a meeting at the Arsenal the following morning; I have been helping him with the design of a pump. The manager of the Arsenal entertained us to dinner on Sunday night, and we stayed with him overnight, so that we could start early on the pump testing, on Monday morning.'

'It appears you have an excellent alibi, Paolo. We will need to check it though, I'm afraid,' Anthony replied.

'I can take you to the palace today if you like. The council meetings are all recorded. The clerk will show you the minutes. And then we can go to the Arsenal.'

'That will be very helpful. I like to see every angle of a problem. We are informed that you were in regular contact with heretics and that you deny the immortality of the soul. Is that true?'

'I am in contact with many great intellectuals. Often I simply can't reconcile reason, the power of our God-given intellect, with blind faith. Unfortunately, heresy has become a matter of questioning anything that may affect the power of the church. Certainly I deny the immortality of the soul.'

'How can you possibly, as a holy man, deny the immortal soul?' Anthony asked.

'How can you assert it? I see no grand purpose in the soul. Where does it come from? Where does it go when I die? What does it do? We are sentient beings with eyes to see, fingers to touch, ears to hear, noses to smell, and tongues to taste. We have brains to think and examine the things that our senses detect. What would my immortal soul do after my death, without eyes to see or a brain to think? When did my soul arrive? Did it come from my mother and father? Was it delivered to me by an angel at the moment of birth? Earlier, perhaps, while I was in the womb? There are a great horde of people who have descended from Adam and Eve. What are all their souls to do? Are they reincarnated, as some believe? Does God make new souls?'

'So what do you believe happens when you die?' Anthony asked.

'Creation and the creator will absorb me. I will become at one with God. I cannot imagine that God is partitioned into tiny identities that represent Paolo Sarpi, Anthony Standen, Hugh O'Neill, and every other person who ever lived. Whatever Paolo Sarpi is, will have served its purpose, I pray. The soul is a device by which the church exerts its authority. "Do as I bid, or your soul will endure the fires of hell." That is the only purpose that I recognise for an immortal soul.'

'I see, or rather I don't,' Anthony said, running his fingers through his hair. 'Are you an atheist?'

'No, I am a Catholic. When I look at the stars in the heavens, or the flowers in the meadow, or children playing, I marvel at the wonder of God. There is a limit to faith, but there is a limit too for reason. There is more to creation than we can possibly understand.'

'But the Catholic Church holds you to be a heretic, yet you say you are a Catholic.'

'Religion has existed as long as man. It provides the framework of law which enables society to function. It is necessary. Unfortunately, the church has become corrupt; the Lutheran reformation has been the result.'

'Yes, I see,' Anthony said. 'Quis custodiet ipsos custodes?'

'Quite so, and the wars of religion are an abomination. What do you know of the Council of Trent?'

'I've heard of it, but I couldn't tell you much about it.'

'I am writing a history of it. The council sat for three

long sessions over eighteen years. The objective was to bring the fractured church of Christ together again. It set about reforming the Catholic Church and providing clarification of Catholic doctrine. The end result was effectively no significant change. The Lutherans were not appeased. We still permit a bishop to have multiple sees, and we must still believe in transubstantiation. That is that the bread and wine physically become the body and blood of Christ. So Christians are still burning Christians. I find it hard to bear.'

'So do I.'

'Why don't we do something less intellectually challenging? Shall I take you to the Palazzio, and the Arsenal?' Paolo suggested, standing up from his chair. Hugh stood and, as Anthony rose, his gaze ran across Paolo's bookshelves.

'The Supper of Ashes, is this about burning people?' Anthony asked.

'Quite the opposite. The ashes referred to concern the myth of a man who had made an animal sacrifice on the summit of Mount Olympus. He wrote some words in the cold ashes before descending. He returned the following year, and found the ashes completely undisturbed, and the words just as he wrote them. The calm at the summit of the mountain is a metaphor for the divine. Dear Giordano was hoping for the reconciliation of man with God, and an end of religious war. It is very poignant though...'

'Absolutely, I have seen such atrocities committed by Catholic against Protestant and Protestant against Catholic. I had the honour to meet William of Orange when I was young. You might imagine that he was the very definition of Protestant, yet he remained a Catholic and abhorred the notion that a king should dictate what religion a man should follow. He was the greatest man I have met.' Anthony smiled wistfully, as there was a knock on the door.

'What is it, Daniela?' Paolo asked, as the door opened.

'I beg your pardon, sir, I just wondered if these gentlemen will be joining you for lunch?' the housekeeper enquired. Paolo looked to Anthony and Hugh, and they both shook their heads.

'No thank you, Daniela, but could you defer it until, say, two o'clock? We are just going to visit the Palazzo and the Arsenal, and then I will take lunch.'

They walked the short distance from Paolo's house to the Doge's Palace. They signed in at the guardroom and Paolo asked the sentry to turn to the entries on the pages for the eleventh of July. He pointed out his signature to Anthony and Hugh. Anthony asked to see the following pages. There were very few entries on Sunday, but Paolo's signature appeared again on Monday. Paolo then led them along a corridor and up a broad flight of steps, along another corridor, and then into the clerk's office. The clerk nearest the door stood up from his desk as Paolo entered. He was middle-aged, of medium height and build, with receding black hair. He seemed to squint a little.

'Is that Brother Sarpi, sir?'

'Yes, good morning, Giovani. You should rest your eyes from time to time, you know. Could you show these gentlemen the minutes of the council I attended, on the eleventh of July, please.'

'If you say so, sir.' The clerk opened a cupboard beside his desk and took out a bundle of papers tied with ribbon. He undid the ribbon and searched through the papers until he found the relevant document. 'There you are, sir.' Paolo took the paper and handed it to Anthony.

'Yes, I see, and you seem to have had quite a lot to say.'

'Thank you, Giovani.' Paolo said to the clerk. They left the palace and walked to the quayside, where Paolo spoke with a gondolier.

'It is not too far to the Arsenal, but it is easier by gondola. Step aboard, gentlemen.' Once they were all seated, the gondolier pushed off from the quayside and they were soon slipping through the water.

'Have you ever seen a city like this, Hugh? I've heard about it, but I thought it must be an exaggeration.'

'Never. Its beauty has no equal, so it doesn't.' They sat in silence as the gondola glided past the Doge's Palace. Paolo sat in the bow, facing aft, smiling as his unexpected visitors gazed around them, mouths agape. A dozen gondolas were touting for fares at the palace, their bows held against the quay by the practiced light sculling of their gondoliers. They continued for a few hundred yards, then turned into a narrow canal to their left. The muffled sound of a baritone singing drifted across the water to them, accompanied by the plucking of a lute. The song got louder, as ahead of them a gondola emerged from under a low bridge. Anthony was captivated by the gentle curve of the bridge and its reflection in the water, forming an image that reminded him of pursed lips, the lower lip

71

trembling in the other gondola's wake. The baritone didn't take his eyes off the young brunette as the gondolas passed. A splash of water from the oar of the passing gondola landed on Antony's cheek, just as they passed under the bridge. The water trickled onto Anthony's lips, and he tasted Francesca's salty tears again. 'Anthony, is it coming with us you are?' Anthony looked up to see Hugh and Paolo standing on the quay. He clutched the sides of the gondola, stood up, and stepped ashore.

'Would you wait please, we shall not be long,' Paolo asked the gondolier, who nodded assent. They stepped ashore, and Paolo led them a short distance to the guardhouse. Once again, Paolo was clearly well known to the guard, and they checked the register for the second of August, which contained both Paolo's and Galileo's signatures. The guardsman was reluctant to permit Anthony and Hugh entry, so a messenger was sent to fetch the manager. While they waited, one sentry remained with them, whilst another inspected barges, before waving them through towards a building that was as large as a palace, but plain. After ten or fifteen minutes, a man came striding towards the guardhouse from the vast building.

'Brother Sarpi, we weren't expecting you today. What a pleasant surprise.'

'Signore Ferreti, would you mind telling these gentlemen where I was on Saint Eusebius's Day please.'

'I remember it well. The pump has proved to be a great success. You were here with Professor Galilei resolving the teething problems we had with the prototype. You both dined with me on the Sunday evening, just a small token of my gratitude, and we all worked on the pump again on Monday morning.'

'Thank you. Now are you satisfied, gentlemen?'

'Yes, I think so,' Anthony replied and Hugh nodded. 'Judging only by what we can see from here, you seem to have a very impressive operation, Signore Ferreti.'

'Thank you. I'm afraid that, much as I would be proud to do so, I cannot show you around. Many aspects of our operation are secret. We wouldn't want other nations to launch a warship every day.'

'Did you say a warship every day?' Anthony gasped.

'Yes. We have around sixteen thousand workers, but some of the processes used are secret. I'm sorry.' They thanked the manager and returned to their waiting gondola which, dropped them back by Saint Mark's Square.

'Surprisingly, it has been a pleasure to meet you, gentlemen; I can't say that of all my inquisitors. Are you sure that you wouldn't like to join me for lunch?'

'No, but thank you, Paolo. I think we are satisfied of your innocence,' Anthony said, glancing at Hugh, who nodded, 'but we still have a killer to catch. The sooner we do that, the sooner I get home to my wife and children.' They shook hands and Paolo walked back to his house while Anthony and Hugh went back to the quay to wait for the ferry. 'Well Hugh, did you have any sense that Paolo was lying?'

'That I did not. There was nothing of the lying about him. Utterly sincere to me, he seemed.'

'Me too. Well, let's get back to Padua and see what

suspects we have.'

CHAPTER SIX

They arrived back in Padua the following day, Sunday, the sixth of September. As it was getting late, and they were tired, they went straight to the monastery. The following morning, they went to see the chancellor. Insert chapter six text here.

'Welcome back. What did you think of Venice?'

'I would like to visit again when I have time. Do you have the list?'

'Yes,' the chancellor said, handing Anthony a sheet of paper. 'I have crossed out those we know to be dead, plague victims mostly. We have also been able to eliminate most of the ex-students who remain in the city, apart from an Englishman, Mark Brown. He was an exceptional student, but rather sickly. My clerk spoke to him and he had a bad attack of diarrhoea on Saint Benedict's Day, and a fever for a week around Saint Eusebius's Day. There is Gino Torelli from Monselice, then there are two in Florence, Andrea Satoro and Mario Tuscani.'

'Thank you, chancellor,' Anthony said, taking the list. 'Shall we go, Hugh?'

'I think so, thank you, chancellor,' Hugh added as they shook hands and left.

'This Gino Torelli from Monselice, he might have been a choirboy; it gives him a potential motive. We should speak to him. The Englishman sounds too weak.'

'That's fine, so it is, although I still don't see why he would go in for this sun and Earth routine, nor why he would kill the priest in Ferrara as well.'

'Perhaps he wanted, in some perverted way, to make it look like a series of murders associated with heliocentricity, in order to divert attention from the abuse motive.'

'Well, straight to him, it led us. That wouldn't have been very clever, for a man with the university behind him now, would it? Could a university graduate be that stupid? Anyway, I agree we need to speak to him, but first we should be checking out this Mark Brown, right here in Padua. Sickly he may be, but an accomplice he may have had with him. After that, on the way to Florence, Gino we can call on.'

'You're right, Hugh. Let's do that.'

They found the clockmaker's workshop above which Mark Brown rented rooms. They entered and found the clockmaker at work behind a bench. There were shelves on which a variety of clocks stood. There were large wooden cased clocks and smaller brass ones. They ticked a discordant cacophony. There were several portraits hanging on the walls, and about a dozen clocks on cabinets around the room. The clockmaker looked up.

'Can I help you? Are you looking for a clock?' he shouted.

'No, we believe an Englishman lives here, Mark Brown. Is he in?' Anthony asked, raising his voice to be heard above the ticking.

'Yes, he's in. Through that door and up the stairs,' he pointed. They went up the stairs and knocked on the only door on a small landing. There was the sound of footsteps, and a thin, pale man, who should have been twenty-two, but looked at least thirty, opened the door. He was below average height.

'Are you after portraits?'

'No, are you Mark Brown?' Anthony asked. The man nodded. He was wearing a paint-spattered smock over breeches. 'Then you will have been asked where you were on Saint Benedict's Day and Saint Eusebius's Day by the chancellor's clerk. We are conducting an investigation on the authority of Pope Paul and would like to ask you some more questions. May we come in?'

'Certainly.' Brown closed the door behind them as Anthony and Hugh stepped inside. There was a chair in front of an easel, and three other chairs in a row against one wall. Paintings covered the walls, all in the same hand. There were both portraits and landscapes. Anthony recognised a view of the Thames painted from the Southbank, looking towards the Tower. He shuddered a little. There were several scenes of Padua. He recognised a portrait of Galileo, but did not know who the other portraits were of. The floor around the easel was scattered with jars of paint, brushes, and a palette knife. The floorboards were spattered with a spectrum of colours. Brown dragged two of the chairs from their place by the wall, placing one on either side of the easel, to face the chair a sitter would use. 'Please sit down. I'm afraid I can't offer you anything. I wasn't expecting guests.' Brown sat in the sitter's chair opposite the easel. Anthony and Hugh sat in the chairs to either side.

'So, you're an artist?' Anthony said.

'Yes, I do reasonably well making portraits. Anybody who can afford a clock can afford to preserve their likeness for posterity. I get quite a few referrals from my landlord, Signore Monsini. How can I help you? I told the clerk I was ill.'

'So we understand. Didn't anyone visit you?'

'The apothecary came around on Saint Benedict's Day with a tonic. It made me sleep for two days.'

'Which apothecary?'

'The one opposite the university library.'

'And did anyone see you whilst you had the fever around Saint Eusebius's Day?'

'No, I didn't get out of bed at all for a few days, except to use the chamber pot. Signore Monsini kindly cancelled the appointments I had with sitters.'

'Your Italian is excellent, but I understand you're English. What brought you to Padua, and where are you from in England?'

'I came to study and fell in love with the city. The climate here is so much better than in England. It may not seem so, but it is better for my health. I was born in London.'

'I am myself from East Molsey, near Hampton Court, where my father was a lawyer. What did your father do?'

'I never knew my father. He was a diplomat from France who seduced my mother. She was in service at Queen Elizabeth's court. He had to return to France before she knew she was pregnant. My mother had to leave court, her prospects damaged.'

'I see. Then how could you afford to study at Padua?'

'My mother married the landlord of a successful inn, and I started selling portraits when I was thirteen.'

'Do you believe the Earth is the centre of the universe?'

'Of course it is,' Brown said, standing up. He paced towards the wall before turning to face them. He took a deep breath and raised his hands above his head, as if to God. 'At that time Joshua spoke to the Lord in the day when the Lord gave the Amorites over to the sons of Israel, and he said in the sight of Israel, Sun, stand still at Gibeon, and Moon, in the Valley of Aijalon. And the sun stood still, and the moon stopped, until the nation took vengeance on their enemies. That's Joshua chapter ten, verses twelve to fourteen,' he added in a calmer voice, as he returned to his chair and sat down. 'It is dangerous to think other than as laid out in the holy scriptures.'

'I see. The sun stopped, so it had to have been moving around the Earth. Professor Galileo Galilei was your tutor, he appears to think otherwise.'

'That is his concern. He was more fun when he played the lute for us in the inn around the corner. His father was a composer, you know.'

'I did notice the lute in his study. Do you have any

plans to leave the city?'

'No, I'm already behind with my portrait work. I'm expecting a wealthy merchant any time now, in fact. Do you have any more questions?'

'I don't. What about you, Hugh?'

'Your step-father's inn. What name did it have?' Hugh asked.

'The Mitre, in Hatton Garden,' Brown replied.

'Have you ever been to Venice?' Anthony asked.

'No, but I'd like to go. I hear it's a wonderful city, I'd love to paint it. I believe the Venetians are rather wealthy too; perhaps I could make a better living than here. It's a thought.'

'Have you heard of a man called Sarpi?'

'The name is vaguely familiar. Let me think a moment. Yes, I do believe Galileo mentioned him. He's a friend of his, I think. Why do you ask?'

'It doesn't matter.'

'That is intriguing.'

'Well, good luck with your client. We'll be off now,' Anthony said, getting up from the chair. When they had left the clockmakers, Anthony turned to Hugh. 'What did you think, Hugh? Did you think he was telling the truth?'

'The only doubt I had was when he said it was an innkeeper that his mother married. That's why I asked himself about that, to see if there was any hesitation about naming the inn. But there was not.'

'Well, if he's from London, he would know plenty of inns, without necessarily having been brought up in one.'

'To be sure, but he doesn't appear to have the strength to carry a body and place it on the bales of straw, does he now?'

'No. Let's go and find that apothecary.'

They found the apothecary opposite the library. As soon as they entered the shop, a wave of aromas hit them. Anthony closed his eyes and tried to identify the aromas, like tasting a wine. There was turmeric, also rosemary and thyme. He thought he could smell oregano, then sage certainly, and perhaps cinnamon. He opened his eyes. Directly ahead of him was a counter running three-quarters of the width of the shop. There was a set of weighing scales, a pestle and mortar, and an open book lying on the counter. The book had text on one page and an illustration of a plant on the other. Directly behind the gap in the counter there was a curtain, which presumably hid a doorway to a room at the back. Behind the counter stood shelving stacked with ceramic jars, each etched with a Latin inscription. He scanned them and found the source of some of the aromas he had identified. The wall to his left was lined with bookshelves. Along with books, there were several preserved creatures, birds, lizards and snakes. The wall to his right was covered in wood panelling. There was a hook on which hung a full-length leather coat with a hood. Into the hood was sewn the beaked mask of a plague doctor. An old, grey-haired man with a stoop appeared through the curtain. As the curtain fell back into place, Anthony saw a laboratory behind the shop that reminded him of the Duke of Tuscany's alchemy laboratory.

'How can I help you, gentlemen?'

'Do you know Mark Brown, an Englishman and portrait painter, who lives above the clockmaker?'

'Yes, he is a regular customer, poor fellow.'

'Did you deliver a tonic to him on Saint Benedict's Day?'

'Why do you ask?'

'We are special investigators commissioned by Pope Paul.'

'Oh dear, in that case, let me have a look in my order book.' He turned and took down a large leather-bound book from the shelves behind him. He flicked through the pages. 'Yes, here it is. I brewed him an infusion of yarrow, elderflower and white-willow bark. I included some valerian, to help him sleep. He said he had a high fever.'

'Did he appear to you to have a high fever?'

'Well, he did look flushed. I didn't touch him. Have you any idea how many apothecaries have died in the plague?'

'What time did you deliver the infusion?'

'Nine o'clock in the morning, by the clocks in the shop he lives above.'

'Thank you. I think that will be all,' Anthony said, then he and Hugh left the shop. 'So he may not have had a fever, and he could have easily ridden to Monselice by late afternoon. He could have done it, Hugh.'

'Technically he could, but he doesn't look capable, does he now? And what's his motive? He didn't seem deranged about the sun theory. So you saw his room, he doesn't look like he's profited from stolen treasures, does he now?'

'No, you're right. We must speak to Gino Torelli in Monselice next, then proceed to Florence and interview the other two, Satoro and Tuscani. It's not yet noon, I think we could reach Florence in three or four days' hard riding.'

The church bell was striking three o'clock in the afternoon when they reached Monselice. It was a picturesque town, dominated by a rocky outcrop with a castle at the top.

'I imagine from the castle you can see Venice, Padua, perhaps all the way to Bologna,' Anthony mused.

'That's for sure now.'

In Piazza Mazzini, the main square, they asked directions for the Torelli farm, and were told it was two miles down the road towards Ferrara, on the right. They rode out of the square in the direction indicated. The outskirts soon gave way to open countryside, with a few isolated buildings, but nothing giving the impression of a farm. After a quarter of an hour or so, they saw a large farmhouse in the distance. As they got closer, they could see smoke coming from the chimney. A hundred yards or so, farther on, they came across the corner of a stone wall. The wall perpendicular to the road stretched off into the distance towards a copse. To the left of the wall was a large field. Anthony could just make out two men in the distance who may have been picking crops. From the corner, the wall ran parallel with the road. They continued to ride until they reached a gate. There was a wooden sign on the gatepost. It was coated in moss, but they could just make out Torelli Farm. They opened the gate, rode through, and shut it behind them. As they entered the farmyard, a young man in his mid-twenties was lifting large sacks onto the back of a cart, as if they were bags of feathers.

'Are you Gino?' Anthony called out.

'I am. Do you want some onions?'

'No, thank you. We are special investigators, appointed by Pope Paul. I am Sir Anthony Standen and this is Earl Hugh O'Neill of Tyrone. We want to ask you a few questions.' They dismounted and approached Gino and the cart.

'Heavens above, you've come a long way to do the pope's bidding. Ask away. You don't mind if I finish loading, do you. I want to be away to Ferrara first thing in the morning.'

'What business do you have there?'

'There's a market, and I have surplus produce. I'm going to sell my onions, beans and cabbages. A couple of crates of chickens too, if I'm lucky.'

'Do you go to Ferrara often?'

'I do when I can't sell all my produce in Monselice. Ferrara is the next-nearest market. I met my wife there, so it has a special appeal for me. Is that all you wanted to know?'

'Were you a choirboy here, when you were young?'

'I try not to think about that. It still gives me nightmares.'

'Did you hear that Father Valenti is dead?'

'No, but I can't say I'm sorry.'

'The floor of your cart has earth on it, so it does,' Hugh remarked.

'The vegetables have come from the soil. They don't grow on trees, you know. Of course the cart's got earth in it, chicken shit too. There, that's the last one. Do you want to come inside for a bowl of soup? Juliet makes wonderful soup. I hope you've got some better questions. We get little entertainment out here.' They followed Gino over to the farmhouse, and in through the kitchen door. There was a huge fire blazing, and a lamb carcass roasting on a spit, turned by a dog wheel. A woman in her late-teens or early twenties got up from a chair as they entered and put her sewing down on the large kitchen table. As she turned towards them, Anthony thought she might be pregnant. She reminded him of Francesca. Anthony stood staring at her, but thinking of Francesca, hoping she was well, and hoping she had forgiven him. Juliet had lightly tanned hands and face, and long black hair. Her eyes were brown and glowing. She wore a cotton dress that was tight around her middle, and her figure had the gentle, pleasing curves of a swift ship. 'These gentlemen have come from Pope Paul to ask me some questions, Juliet. What do you think of that, eh?'

'Oh my lord, whatever for?' Juliet exclaimed.

'Don't be alarmed, Signora, we are asking many people questions. I'm sure you have nothing to fear,' Anthony said.

'You may as well sit down,' Gino suggested. 'Would you pour us all some soup please, darling? I'd do it, but I'm knackered.' Hugh, Anthony, and Gino sat down at the kitchen table. This would seat a dozen people comfortably, Anthony thought.

'I'll get right to the point. Where were you on Saint Eusebius's Day this August?' Anthony asked.

'I was in Ferrara, selling my produce at the market. I

stayed overnight there in the Cross Keys Inn. You can ask the landlord. I stay there whenever I'm at the market.'

'And where were you on Saint Benedict's Day?'

'I was here with Juliet.'

'Can you confirm that, signora?' Anthony asked, as she put the bowls of soup on the table.

'Not only me,' Juliet replied, smiling, her hands stroking her baby bump. 'We have only two farmhands to help us. Since Gino's father died last year, he's worked so hard. But I remember St. Benedict's Day very well. He wasn't as tired as usual, you see. Are you both family men?'

'Yes.' They both nodded.

'Well, that was the only time for weeks you see, and within a couple of weeks, I knew I was pregnant. Here is the proof you seek.'

'Good lord,' Anthony said blushing, and quickly asked another question. 'Gino, you studied mathematics and science with Professor Galileo Galilei, I believe?'

'That's right.'

'Do you believe in heliocentricity?'

'I understand the theory, but if it's a question of belief, I believe in the holy scriptures. Anything else is heresy, isn't it?'

'Er yes. There is something that puzzles me,' Anthony continued. 'With a university education, why did you take on the farm?'

'I was in my final year at university when I received news that my mother, my two sisters and my three younger brothers had died from the plague. By the time I got back here, my father was quietly drinking himself to death. I couldn't save him, but I took over working the farm.'

'Your father must have been making a good living from the farm, to send you to university. If you don't mind me saying so, it looks a little run down now. Couldn't you have made a better living from your studies?'

'I thought about selling the farm, but buyers were in short supply. Not only did I lose my family to the plague, but a quarter of our customers too. Besides, as you said, I studied science and mathematics. I did that because they interested me, but there's no money in it. Look at poor Galileo. He's probably the most intelligent, inventive and wise man who ever lived, but he's deeply in debt and can barely support his family. If I'd had my head screwed on, I would have studied art or divinity. That's where the money is, in the church and the artists it patronises.'

'Have you ever been to Venice?' Anthony asked.

'As a matter of fact, I have. It's a wonderful place. I must take you there one day, Juliet, when we can afford some more help on the farm. It was during a long vacation at university. Galileo spoke of it often, and I wanted to see it. I told him I was planning to go there during the vacation, and he gave me the name of a friend of his. He said he would put me up for a week or two. He did. He was an absolutely wonderful man. We sat up late into the night talking about science, philosophy, history, religion, art, you name it. You will never meet a more generous, kind, clever and gentle man.'

'Paolo Sarpi?' Anthony asked.

'Yes, have you met him?'

'Yes, and I agree with you. Have you kept in touch?'

'We exchange letters at Christmas, that's all. I'm afraid mine are rather short and dull. I write about the crops, the markets, that sort of thing. I'll have more to write about this Christmas,' Gino said, squeezing Juliet's hand.

'Do you still have Paolo's letters?'

'Yes, I think so, they're in a drawer in our bedroom I think.'

'Would you mind fetching them, please?'

'No, but whatever for?'

'I'm afraid I cannot say.'

'Very well,' Gino said, as he got up and left the kitchen.

'Whatever is this about, sir?' Juliet asked.

'We cannot say. But I'm sure you have nothing to fear. We are questioning several people.' There was an uncomfortable silence until Gino returned, holding half a dozen letters. He placed them on the table in front of Anthony. Anthony picked them up and started reading.

'Do you mind if I take these with me? I shall return them to you as soon as I can.'

'No, I don't mind.'

'Well, do you have any questions, Hugh?'

'I don't. I think you've covered it, so you have. We can make enquiries at the Crossed Keys, and then continue our journey.'

'Sir Anthony, Earl Hugh, it is already getting dark. Why don't you spend the night here? We have spare rooms. We have plenty of lamb, vegetables, and we have cider. My farmhands, Milo and Giuseppe will be coming in from the lower field soon. They'll not have met a knight and an earl before. It will enhance my status no end.'

'I'm not sure, we have a long journey.'

'Well, you won't get far tonight, and I'll be up with the first cock-crow in the morning to set off for market. I'll wake you.'

'What do you think, Hugh?'

'My mouth has been watering at the scent of that lamb, so it has, for the last hour.'

'Excellent. I'll put your horses in the stable.'

'I'll lay the table for six,' Juliet said.

Hugh and Anthony had been riding for an hour towards Ferrera by the time the upper limb of the sun rose above the horizon.

'What did you think of Gino, Hugh?'

'I liked him. Clearly, he had suffered abuse from the priest, so he has a motive on him. But with a child on the way and a lovely, young wife, I simply don't see him as a serial killer. To be sure, there is simply no reason for the sun and earth thing.'

'I agree. Juliet was convincing with her alibi, although loyal wife and all that.'

'That's fine so, but we weren't expected. It couldn't have been staged, so it couldn't.'

'He was in the near vicinity of both murders. Let's reserve judgement until we hear what the innkeeper at the Crossed Keys has to say.' They reached Ferrara by mid-morning and went straight to the Crossed Keys. The innkeeper was inserting a tap into a barrel behind the bar.

'Good morning, gentlemen. What will you have?'

'Bread, cheese, and wine for me, please,' Anthony said.

'I'll be having the same, please,' Hugo added. The innkeeper poured two goblets of red wine and passed them across the bar. He went through a door and came back a few minutes later with plates of bread and cheese.

'Thank you. We stayed last night with Gino Torelli and his wife, a lovely couple. I believe he stays here when he comes to market.'

'That's right. He met Juliet here, as a matter of fact. I lost a great waitress, and he gained a beautiful wife.'

'And mother to be.'

'So I heard.'

'He said he was here on Saint Eusebius's Day in August. But Juliet said he went to Padua. They had quite a little squabble about it. Young love, you know what it's like.'

'Well I can settle that.' The innkeeper reached for a notebook on a shelf behind the bar. He leafed through a few pages. 'He was here all right.'

'No chance he could have slipped out during the night?'

'That's an odd question to ask, but no, none at all. When all the guests have gone to their rooms, I lock the doors and don't unlock them until the morning.'

'And where is the key kept?'

'On my belt. What is this?'

'Oh nothing, just trying to settle an argument. This wine is excellent.' Anthony and Hugh finished their wine and lunch, paid the innkeeper, and got back on the road again. They settled into a canter.

'This trip seems to have done wonders for Lightning. I haven't been riding him so much, with all the work to do on the vineyard. He's really regaining his old fitness. Do you think we can reach Bologna by nightfall?'

'It's quite a stretch, but you're right. The miles seem to be shortening,' Hugh shouted above the pounding of the hooves.

They reached Bologna as the sun set on their second day of riding south from Padua, Wednesday, the ninth of September.

'I think this is as far as we can get today, Hugh. Let's go to the monastery San Domenico again, we can be sure of a friendly welcome from Abbot Fontana.'

'That's an excellent idea, so it is. I was thinking the same myself. Those wines, and the feast were exquisite.' They dismounted outside the main door to the monastery, but this time, nobody came rushing out to greet them. 'You certainly get a better reception if you have a cardinal with you, don't you?' Hugh banged his fist on the door. After a few minutes, the door opened, and a monk appeared.

'Oh, I remember, you were here with Cardinal Aldobrandini, just over a week ago,' the monk said, smiling.

'Yes, we are on the pope's business. We'd like to stay the night. Can we see Abbot Fontana?' Hugh asked.

'Of course, come this way. I will have your horses looked after.' The monk led them to the abbot's house.

'Why, Sir Anthony and Earl Hugh, this is a pleasure.

Do you have time for a guided tour of the university in the morning this time?'

'Sadly no, we must be on our way at first light,' Anthony replied.

'And are you still unable to tell me what the urgency of your mission is?'

'I fear not.'

'Very well, but you shall dine with me again. Brother Vitale, would you tell the kitchen that I am entertaining two guests this evening? Ensure that we have a fine selection of our best wines.' The monk bowed and left. A few hours later, Anthony and Hugh made their way to the higher-ranking guest accommodation, where they slept soundly.

They arrived in Florence after two days of hard riding, late on Friday, the eleventh of September. They agreed that the abbey they had stayed in on their last visit paled in comparison to Bologna, so they took rooms at an inn. In the morning they found the residence of Andrea Satoro. Hugh knocked on the door and after a few moments they heard footsteps and a tall, broad, smartly dressed man of about thirty opened the door.

'Good morning. Are you Andrea Satoro?' Anthony asked.

'Yes, and you are?'

'I am Sir Anthony Standen, and this is Hugh O'Neill, Earl of Tyrone.'

'Goodness, you're a long way from home. What can I do for you?'

'We are carrying out an investigation, under the

authority of Pope Paul. May we come in?'

'Certainly.' Andrea led them to his study. It was a large, light, and airy room. There was a big desk with an open notebook, pens and ink pot on the desktop. Bookshelves dominated the wall opposite the door. 'Please sit down,' he said, pulling two chairs from behind the door and positioning them in front of the desk. Andrea sat down behind the desk.

'Can you tell us what you were doing on Saint Benedict's Day, please?' Anthony asked.

'Let me see, yes Saturday the eleventh of July. I was here most of the day.'

'Can anyone vouch for that?'

'Only Nicolaus Copernicus, I'm afraid; my housekeeper had the weekend off.'

'Are you married?'

'No. Perhaps I will marry one day, when the right girl comes along.'

'Nicolaus Copernicus, did you say? That's promising. I think I've heard the name. Where can we find him?' Anthony asked.

'His ashes are in an urn in Frombork Cathedral, in Poland. I'm writing a biography of him. He was the first to challenge Ptolomy's model of the universe.'

'Ah, yes, that's where I've heard of him. So do you believe the Earth is not the centre of the universe?'

'Since you are on the pope's business, I believe that the Earth is the centre of the universe, as set out in the holy scriptures. The fellow was an absolute genius though.'

'What about Saint Eusebius's Day, Sunday the second

of August?'

'My housekeeper has most weekends off, so I just had Nicolaus for company. It's going to be a long book.'

'What about the week after Saint Eusebius's Day?'

'Yes, my housekeeper was back on Monday. On Tuesday I had a meeting with a friend, Mario Francesi. He's been reading my first few chapters. We usually meet in the inn around the corner for a few drinks. The landlord will have a record, I have credit there.'

'If it's not too impertinent, Signor Satoro, do you make your income from writing, or do you have other means at your disposal?'

'So far, writing has cost me far more that it has returned to me. Paper and ink are not cheap. I hope to recover my expenses with the Copernicus biography, if the church will let me publish it, of course. I will be at pains to point out the error of his planetary theories, but you never know. This house was left to me by my late father. I fear I was rather a disappointment to him. He wanted me to study law, but I was more interested in mathematics and science.'

'My father was a lawyer too, and he hoped that I would follow him into it. It was languages with me, that's what fascinated me. So he left you the house. Did he leave you a fortune as well?'

'Yes, but I'm getting through it quite quickly. That's why I'm working so hard on the book.'

'Well, good luck with that. Where can we find your housekeeper, and your friend Francesi?'

'Why do you want to know?'

'We will need to verify that you were where you say

you were, it's just routine.'

'What's this all about?'

'We are not at liberty to say. We can call back with the Swiss Guard if you like.'

'No, that's all right, I'll write their addresses down for you. The inn is the Cantina Locale. Will that be all?' He reached down into a wastepaper basket and pulled out a ball of paper. He unfolded it and wrote down the addresses and handed Anthony the paper.

'Yes, thank you for your time,' Anthony said, getting up. Andrea showed them to the door where they shook hands. Anthony waited until he heard the door close behind him, before turning to Hugh. 'Well if his alibi checks out, it looks like he's in the clear.'

'So it does, although the strength to carry a man and bales of straw he certainly has, so he does. And he's clearly a believer in the sun theory. If it's capital he's short of, perhaps he's behind the art thefts. There we go now, he's bribed the housekeeper, his friend and the innkeeper.'

'Possibly, but he didn't seem to be the sort to me. Did you think he was lying at any point?'

'Only when he said that the Earth was the centre of the universe.'

'Well as we're employed by the pope, he had to say that. Let's check out his story first, and speak to the other suspect in Florence, Mario Tuscani.' They went to the Cantina Locale around the corner. It was busy, but they eventually managed to attract the attention of the innkeeper.

'What can I get you, gentlemen?'

'A flagon of wine, and two goblets please.'

'Coming right up.' The landlord returned a few minutes later with their drinks. 'I haven't seen you in here before. Where are you from?'

'I'm English and my colleague is Irish,' Anthony replied.

'Ah, in the wool trade are you?'

'No, not exactly. Do you know Andrea Satoro and his friend — Mario Tuscani? We believe they drink in here quite often.'

'Yes they do. Signor Satoro's tab is getting rather large. I keep trying to get him to pay, but he always seems to be waiting for an advance from his publisher.'

'Would you be able to tell us if he was drinking in here on the Tuesday after Saint Eusebius's Day? That would be Tuesday the fourth of August?'

'I can, if I look in my book. I'll be back in a moment.' The innkeeper soon returned with his account book. 'Yes that's right, he was here. He must have been with his friend, they got through three flagons of wine. He says it helps him with his inspiration. If he doesn't settle his account soon, I'll help inspire him a bit.' Anthony and Hugh finished their wine and then went to the address of the housekeeper. She confirmed that he had definitely been at home working on his book on the Mondays after both of the murders. They then went to the address of Mario Tuscani, where a neighbour said that he had been out of the city for a few days and was expected back on Monday.

'So is it that we wait here to interview him, or head for Rome?' Hugh asked.

'For the sake of two days, I suggest we wait. It will take time for the cardinal's men to work their way here from Rome, and the more suspects we can eliminate the better. I suggest we go back to the Cantina Locale. It seemed quite a popular place, we might hear some gossip. I'd like to find out who the current Duke of Tuscany is.'

'How does the duke make a difference?'

'You remember I said I was sent to spy on the Duke of Tuscany by Walsingham, because he was thought to be sending aid to Mary Queen of Scots?'

'I do remember that.'

'And that it was here in Florence, where I met and fell in love with Francesca. Well actually I got on very well with Grand Duke Francesco, I liked him. I learnt a lot from his library, particularly his Arabic books, on various subjects including science, mathematics and medicine. Unfortunately, he and his wife Bianca died suddenly. Their symptoms corresponded with arsenic poisoning, and I'm quite certain it was his younger brother Ferdinando who administered it. He usurped the grand duchy from Francesco's son Crown Prince Philip. If Ferdinando is still Grand Duke, then it would be dangerous to be recognised by him. He knew, that I knew he'd done it. I had to flee.'

'When was that?'

'I was here from eighty to eighty-seven.'

'Twenty years ago, that was. Was it an assumed name that you were under?'

'Unfortunately not. I was Sir Anthony Standen because I had saved Mary from death when her husband murdered her secretary. I had to be myself, to secure an introduction from Mary Queen of Scots to Grand Duke Francesco.'

'Well here we are happily going around introducing ourselves, in Florence, you as Sir Anthony Standen, and hoping that the duke doesn't hear about us, because he almost certainly wants you dead, so he does. Clever is that?'

'I'm sorry, it slipped my mind. It was twenty years ago.'

'I'll tell you what we'll be doing. I'll go and eavesdrop in another inn, not the one I drank in as an associate of an enemy of the state. You take yourself back to the inn we're lodging in, and lie low. You can lie low tomorrow too. I'll go and check up on Mario Toscani on Monday, then we'll high-tail it back to Rome.'

'Your Italian isn't as good as mine.'

'There we go now, good enough it is, and I'm not the enemy of the grand duke.'

'I suppose you're right.'

On Sunday night, Hugh was returning from a tour of a few inns, where he had assumed the alias of an Irish cloth merchant. He had learnt that Ferdinando was still the grand duke. In fact, the locals seemed to have a genuinely high regard for Ferdinando. He had ruled mildly, had a genuine interest in the welfare of his subjects, and restored the justice system. He had also revitalised the economy through the Medici bank. Perhaps Anthony was wrong about the arsenic, or perhaps having gained his position through murder, he was atoning for his crime. As Hugh was approaching their inn, a rider in the white habit and black cloak of the Dominicans galloped into the square. Hugh recognised him as Brother Vitale and called out to him. Brother Vitale reined his horse in.

'That's a great hurry you're in brother, where is it you're going?'

'Oh praise the Lord, it's you, Earl O'Neill. I am riding to Rome. They have killed Father Abbot Fontana. It must be satan's work. I have to tell his holiness the pope.'

'Was he burnt on bales of straw, in the church?'

'Yes, how did you know?'

'When was it that he was found?'

'He was found just before dawn, when we went to celebrate lauds, the morning after Saint Cyprians Day. I have ridden all day yesterday, and all day today.'

'You must come with me to see Sir Anthony, himself. We are staying in the inn yonder.'

Anthony was examining Paolo Sarpi's letters to Gino, when there was a knock on his door.

'Anthony, it's Hugh.' Anthony opened the door. 'It was just crossing the square I was, when I recognised Brother Vitale. Abbot Fontana has been murdered, in the usual way, on the night of Saint Cyprians.'

'My god! Come in, sit down, Brother. Tell us what you know.' Brother Vitale sat on the bed, his hands clasped in his lap.

'We found his, I can hardly call it his body, his charred remains, in the chapel when we arrived to celebrate lauds at dawn. There was some straw scattered about, and a circle of earth around him. It must have happened between around two hours after midnight, when matins ended, and dawn for lauds.'

'Have you any idea how someone got into the monastery?'

'The main gate was locked, and there were brothers there overnight, in case someone came seeking help. We found some straw around one of the side gates near the chapel. That gate isn't opened very often, so I went to fetch the key. We found some straw outside as well.'

'That will be how the murderer got in.'

'What should I do now? I've been sent to inform the pope.'

'It's getting late. I suggest we get you a room here tonight. You can continue towards Rome tomorrow. We have to wait until Monday to speak to someone here, then we will follow you,' Anthony murmured, deep in thought.

'Anthony, Ferdinando is still the grand duke. Safe it isn't for you here. It's south with Brother Vitale that you should ride. I'll interview Toscani and then, follow you I will?' Hugh suggested.

'Is he indeed? Yes, that sounds reasonable. Hugh, could you take Brother Vitale to the landlord and see if you can fix him up with a room, then come back here. I think we need to think this over,' Hugh nodded and led Brother Vitale out. Twenty minutes later he knocked, entered and sat down on the bed. Anthony was sitting in a chair by a small writing desk.

'Are those Sarpi's letters to Gino, Anthony?'

'Yes.'

'What is it that you expect to find in them?'

'Nothing, but I'm looking for any ciphers or codes. If invisible ink had been used, it would have been obvious, and he would have denied receiving any letters.'

'What sort of ciphers or codes?'

'I've looked at the dates. This letter is dated the sixth of December. I've looked at every sixth word, and every sixth letter to see if there is any encoded message, but I haven't found anything. I was just starting a frequency analysis.'

'Frequency analysis?'

'Some letters occur more often than others. The letter E is the most frequently occurring letter. All the other letters of the alphabet have a ranking. I was looking to see if there was anything odd about the frequency of letters used.'

'So is there?'

'Not that I can see. They appear to be perfectly innocent letters. Hugh, do you think Brother Vitale could be the murderer? He may have been sent to Rome, or he may be on his way to the next murder.'

'So you saw him, he's a wreck, not a cold-blooded killer, that he isn't. Besides, he's a man of God, more likely to be a victim that the murderer.'

'But burning, Hugh, do you know anyone who has ever used burning as a ritual form of murder, other than the church itself?'

'Well no, if you put it like that. But what about this sun and earth thing? Whoever the murderer is, it's a deep hatred of the church that he has, and it has something to do with the sun and the earth. That's why we're chasing after everyone taught by Galileo, so it is?'

'Yes, you're absolutely right, it's just been a shock. He was such a kind and jovial man, Abbot Fontana. It's knocked me sideways a bit, I suppose.'

'There we go now, there is something in what you said, about him being on the way to the next murder. It was from Rome to Padua that we rode, passing first through Bologna, the scene of the third murder. Then we reached the site of the second murder, Ferrara. We continued northeast to Monselice, the site of the first murder. From there it was a three-hour ride to Padua, or a full day's ride to Venice. So the murderer is working his way from Padua, or possibly Venice, killing on holy nights, towards Rome. And killing in a very distinctive way, so he is. I think Rome is the ultimate target.'

'My god, you have something there, Hugh. We need to warn the cardinal. I don't know how many Swiss guards they have, but they should post some soldiers around the churches and monasteries between here and Rome.'

'To be sure that is what they should do, but I sense this thing somehow started in Rome, and it's going to end in Rome. We may find they want to keep their Swiss guard around them.'

'Then what can we do? We can't guard all these places ourselves. We can't warn them to lock themselves in at night, this man can pick locks. These poor souls are defenceless. But it may start to slow down now.'

'So why do you say that?'

'If the murderer is in Padua or Venice, then he was within a two or three-day ride of Bologna. He could get there and back in a week. The nearer he gets to Rome, the longer it will take him to get to the murder scene, and back again.'

'There he is now,' Hugh said, stroking his beard, 'if

back he needs to get. But this fellow can steal what he needs. He doesn't need to keep his job, or run his business. If he has a cover story to maintain, then has a choice on himself. He can create some plausible alibis for increasingly lengthy business trips, or he can commit himself whole-heartedly to completing his mission. Far from slowing down, the murders may speed up. I think this is a race now, so it is.'

'What can we do, Hugh?'

'Anthony, I'm afraid all we can do is what we are doing. We need to get to Rome and scare the bejesus out of them, and find out what this is really all about. I'll interview Tuscani tomorrow, then ride like the blazes to catch you up. You ride south tomorrow, with Vitale. Agreed?'

'Agreed, Hugh. But I've just had another thought. If he's heading for Rome, and he was in Bologna on Friday, then he might have beaten Vitale here; he would have had a couple of hours start on him. He might be here right now.'

'I doubt that, so I do, not if he's travelling by cart. He's got those bales of straw to move around. He must know he's being hunted by now. If he travels to Rome by the shortest route, and covers the greatest distance he can in a day, then it would be child's play to work out where he will strike next. Also we know he needs to kill on Saint's days. We can lie in wait for him.'

'So he may adopt a zig-zag route. There are many churches between Bologna and Rome, and he may want to savour his revenge against the church, take his time. If he's abandoned the need to get home between murders, he can take the scenic route. Buying some straw here, some brandy kegs there, stealing some treasures somewhere else, then strike again. We're going to need eyes and ears everywhere, we're going to need the full resources of the church to catch him. You're right, I'll make best speed for Rome tomorrow, with Brother Vitale.'

Anthony and Brother Vitale rode in silence through the streets of Florence in the early morning twilight. Only with the open road and the warmth of the rising sun, did Anthony feel like talking.

'I can't keep calling you Brother Vitale, what's your name?'

'That is my name Sir Anthony. I was baptised Rafael, but my name was changed when I joined the monastery.'

'You can call me Anthony, Rafael, Brother Vitale, sorry. It's going to be a long ride to Rome. I'm really sorry about Abbot Fontana, I liked him. I'm sorry he didn't get the chance to show us around Bologna and the university. You're Dominicans aren't you? I have no idea how the different orders work. What is it like to be a Dominican?'

'Joyful. I am not surprised that you liked Abbot Fontana. He often quoted the writings of Saint Catherine of Sienna. "Let us behave like the drunkard who doesn't think of himself, but only of the wine he has drunk, and the wine that remains to be drunk." It is of course the joy to be found in the gospels which is the wine which gladdens the hearts of men. Nevertheless, it is, or rather was, in order to appreciate the similarity, and the superiority of the gospels over wine, that Abbot Fontana thought it important to keep comparing the two, at regular intervals.'

'Perhaps I should read the gospels more.'

'Yes, Anthony. Saint Dominic was always described as joyful and spreading laughter wherever he went. His successor, Blessed Jordan, was the same. There is a story of Blessed Jordan, that when there was bread enough for less than half the number present, he exhorted the brothers to laugh, and by his example, he filled them with great joy and gladness, despite their hunger. A woman nearby rebuked them, as holy men, for merry making. When she learnt that they were filled with the joy of the gospels, despite their hunger, she was deeply moved. She hurried home and brought them some bread, wine and cheese.'

'We stayed at Saint Anthony's in Padua. They were Franciscans, I think.'

'That's right. Saint Anthony was a Franciscan. What do you know about Saint Anthony, Sir Anthony?'

'Nothing at all, I'm ashamed to say.'

'He was born into a wealthy family in Lisbon in 1195, and baptised Ferdinand. He was a pious man and shunned the ambitions that his parents had for him. At fifteen he left home and went to live in an Augustinian monastery. When he was twenty-four, he met five Franciscan monks who were on their way to Morocco, to preach to the Muslims. Five years later, he learnt of that they had been martyred in Morocco. Ferdinand meditated upon their sacrifice and decided to join the Franciscans, changing his name to Anthony. He too set off for Morocco, but he contracted a terrible fever and was unable to preach to the Muslims. He set sail back for Portugal, but a terrible storm blew his ship off course. They were blown ashore on Sicily. There he listened to the preachings of Saint Francis. He meditated upon them and travelled widely around northern Italy and France. He preached with great wisdom, knowledge and fervour, but he lived in poverty and died aged only thirty-six.'

'What would you say are the key differences between the Dominicans and the Franciscans?'

'The Franciscans emphasise simple living, rather more than we do, and from their beginning they have been strong in rooting out heresy. In 1236, Pope Gregory appointed them as inquisitors, along with the Dominicans. It was the Franciscans that wrote the Codex Casanatensis, however.'

'What's that?'

'It's the manual for inquisitors. It details all the forms of torture and how to apply them.'

'Suddenly the joyfulness seems to have drained out of me. How do you reconcile joy with torture?'

'It is to spread the joy of the gospels that we must root out heresy. Don't you see?'

'No, I can't say I do. Can you point me to where exactly in the gospels the use of torture is advocated? I don't recall it coming up in the sermon from the mount. Certainly there seems to be a major difference between the Old and New Testaments, I can imagine there might have been a lot of torture going on in the Old Testament, but I don't see Jesus as someone who would have advocated torture.'

'I shall pray for your soul, Sir Anthony.'

'What about the Servite order? I met a fellow who is a member of the Servite Order.'

'They are much like the Franciscans and Dominicans, but place a greater emphasis on their veneration of Mary and her sorrows.' Anthony and Brother Vitale rode in silence the rest of the way to Siena.

Anthony and Brother Vitale rode out of the gates of the Dominican monastery of Siena, through the enormous Piazza Il Campo, where the annual festivals and horse races were held, and headed south, towards Rome.

'I spent some time in the library last night, Sir Anthony, because I wanted to check my facts.'

'What facts?'

'I will try to answer your question concerning the Old and New Testaments. Jesus was of course a Jew. The Tanakh, or Hebrew bible is what we call the Old Testament. It comprises thirty-nine books, the first five of which were written by Moses. Whenever Jesus referred to the holy scriptures, this is what he meant. So it is right that those scriptures, which Jesus considered holy, retain that status.'

'I suppose that's right. But I cannot believe that Jesus approved of torture. "Let him who is without sin cast the first stone." Isn't that what he said? Why doesn't the Christian Church focus on the gospels, those written by the actual disciples who lived with him, knew him, knew what he believed and preached.'

'The disciples did not write the gospels. They were written around thirty to sixty years after Christ's crucifixion, by leaders of the early church. Certainly they sought to capture the accounts of the original disciples, passed down by word of mouth, but they did not write them. Indeed there were several other gospels, that were not included at all.'

'How could gospels not be included?'

'Because some were contradictory. The church leaders had to decide which accounts were holy scripture, and which were not. There were many councils to debate the matter, the principle ones being the Council of Nicea in 325A.D. and the Council of Constantinople in 381A.D. They reached the conclusion as to which books should be included. The Holy Bible, as we know it, the Vulgate Bible, was assembled by Saint Jerome around 400A.D., with thirty-nine books of the Old Testament, and twenty-seven of the New Testament.'

'Why weren't the gospels written in Jesus's lifetime? He was the son of God. He had something new and important to say. Why wasn't anyone writing it down then?'

'We don't know the occupations of all the disciples, but most of them seemed to be fishermen. They were probably illiterate.'

'What about Matthew, the tax collector? He would have been able to write, wouldn't he?'

'Oh yes, certainly the tax collector would have been literate.'

'Then why didn't he keep a diary? Why didn't Jesus, or one of the other disciples, suggest he wrote it all down for posterity?'

'Perhaps they thought that word of mouth was the best

way.'

'You've already said that many of the gospels are contradictory. That's where leaving it decades before asking around, asking the people who had been there, to find out what they remembered, and only then writing it down gets you. It leads to these church councils deciding what they think should be included, and what might be best left out.'

'I do see your point, Sir Anthony.'

'I'd like to read all the gospels. Do you know where the others are?'

'I have no idea. I suppose they might be in the pope's library.'

'When we get there, I expect to be rather busy. If I can get you in, Rafael, would you have a look and see if you can find them?'

'It will be locked, surely?'

'That won't be a problem.'

Anthony and Brother Vitale were approaching Rome and Anthony's mind turned again to his Roman Catholic upbringing.

'You said the other day that Jesus was Jewish. I associate Jesus with love; kindness; charity; thankfulness to God and joy. Was Jesus creating a new religion or urging people to be better Jews?'

'That's quite an interesting question. The defining elements of Christianity, I suppose, are baptism and the miracle of bread becoming the body of Christ, and wine becoming his blood.'

'Baptism is a development of ceremonial washing,

which is an important element of many religions including Judaism. The last supper is, though, quite unique I suppose.' Anthony mused.

'It is unique in that the bread actually becomes Christ's body and the wine his blood. In Genesis chapter fourteen, Melchizedek, the high priest of Salem, blessed Abraham and gave him bread and wine as a symbol of the Holy Spirit.'

'So when did Christianity become distinct and evangelical? When did the passion of men like Saint Anthony and those five Franciscan martyrs develop? When did it become necessary to go abroad and convert men to be charitable, kind, loving Christians rather than, say, charitable, kind, loving Muslims?'

'Soon after Christ's resurrection, Matthew chapter twenty-eight verse nineteen. "Go forth therefore and make all nations my disciples; baptise men everywhere in the name of the Father and the Son, and the Holy Spirit, and teach them to observe all that I have commanded you." That is when it started, Sir Anthony.'

'Yes, I see. I still wish that Matthew had written it all down at the time though.'

CHAPTER SEVEN

Anthony and Brother Vitale continued south towards Rome, stopping only to water and feed the horses, and to rest overnight. They arrived in Rome at dusk on Thursday, the seventeenth of September. They went directly to the pope's residence in the Quirinal palace, and a sentry escorted them to Cardinal Aldobrandini. The cardinal paced his study as Brother Vitale gave his account of the discovery of Abbot Fontana.

'What do you make of this, Sir Anthony?'

'The locations of the murders are leading to Rome, Your Eminence. If the murderer was based in Padua—'

'Or Venice.'

'Or Venice, then if he continues towards Rome, he can no longer return to Padua or Venice. He is now committed to completing his mission, whatever that is.'

'How did your interrogation of Sarpi go?'

'He has cast-iron alibis for the first two murders, so

does Galileo.'

'He may have had an accomplice.'

'Possibly, but neither Hugh nor I can see any kind of motive for him.'

'Where is Earl O'Neill?'

'He stayed in Florence to interview Mario Tuscani, who was away when I left with Brother Vitale. He'll be on his way here by now. How are the other suspects' alibis stacking up?'

'We have as many of the Swiss Guard as we can spare, working their way through the interviews. They have fanned out in pairs from Rome. We have given each pair a cage of two homing pigeons, with instructions to send a message if they discover anything significant. So far, every suspect has a good alibi.'

'Homing pigeons, that's a good idea. Do you have a map, Your Eminence, covering the area from Rome to Bologna?' Cardinal Aldobrandini went to his bookshelves and pulled out a scroll. He placed it on his desk, unrolled it, and placed a paperweight at one end, and a bible on the other edge. 'Here is Monselice, site of the first murder,' Anthony said, pointing at the map. 'There is Ferrera, and here is Bologna. It is possible that the murderer will now continue towards Rome, murdering priests on the nights of saint's days. We know when he was in Bologna, so we can estimate where he may have reached by each saint's day and post guards outside the churches. He will know we can do this, so Hugh and I think he may take a zig-zag route. Homing pigeons could be vital for alerting us to where and when his latest murder was. If we know that, we can guess where he is most likely to strike next, and be waiting for him.'

'Our resources are already stretched. What do you think is the priority, interviewing suspects, or posting guards on churches?' asked Cardinal Aldobrandini.

'If we are right, and the killer has been working from Padua, or Venice, towards Rome, then Hugh and I have already interviewed the remaining suspects between Venice, Padua and Florence. I suggest our priority is to know where he is, rather than who he is.'

'Putting guards on churches will arouse fear. We could cause panic.'

'If I may, Your Eminence,' Brother Vitale interrupted. 'I think the dreadful nature of these murders is already causing panic. Rumours had reached us in San Domenico, of the events in Monselice and Ferrara, the day before Abbot Fontana was murdered. We had taken additional precautions, but our locks were useless.'

'Very well. I will send messengers out with fresh instructions for the Swiss Guard. We have six pairs of guards with pigeons. Where do you suggest we should position them?' Cardinal Aldobrandini enquired. Anthony looked at the map.

'He struck on Saint Cyprian's day in Bologna. When is the next saint's day?'

'Saint John Chrysostom was last Sunday, Saint Cornelius was yesterday. Saint Januarius is on Saturday, Saint Andrew is on Sunday and Saint Matthew on Monday.'

'So he may already have struck again, possibly twice. He's had six days since killing Abbot Fontana in Bologna. In a cart, he could travel thirty miles a day. He may already have travelled a hundred and eighty miles.' Anthony took a piece of ribbon lying on the Cardinal's desk and measured off 180 miles from the map's scale, and placed one end of the ribbon on Bologna. 'I suggest we should assume he could have reached Orte by now. We should create an outer line of guards at Terni, Orte and Viterbo, and an inner line at Fiano Romano, Sutri and Bracciano.'

'We shall have it done. You and Brother Vitale look exhausted. I shall arrange some refreshment for you and rooms here. We shall talk again in the morning.'

On Friday, Anthony was summoned to Cardinal Aldobrandini's rooms.

'I would like to hear a full account of your progress with the suspects you have interviewed, Sir Anthony. Please sit down.' Anthony sat down in a chair in front of the cardinal's large, leather-topped desk.

'Of course, Your Eminence. First, we went to Venice and interviewed Sarpi. He had cast-iron alibis for both murders, which we checked with several witnesses. They also put Galileo in the clear.'

'He may have accomplices. I wouldn't expect him to dirty his own hands.'

'Perhaps, but we have no evidence of it.' Anthony told the cardinal what they knew about Mark Brown and then Gino Torelli. The cardinal listened attentively before asking another question.

'Does he have a motive?'

'Not one that matches the style of the murders, Your Eminence.'

'Which means what, exactly?'

'Well, I'm not sure how to say this, Your Eminence,'

'Speak plainly, Sir Anthony.'

'Very well. In Monselice we spoke with Father Valenti's deacon, Cesare Pelisi. He is a short, weak hunchback with a limp and quite incapable of the murders. What struck us as odd is that Father Valenti's death did not upset him at all. He explained that Valenti abused choirboys.'

'It is rare and unfortunate, but some do struggle with the vow of celibacy. Why did he not report it to Bishop Martino?'

'Well, Your Eminence, there is no easy way to explain. Bishop Martino is also an abuser of choirboys.'

'That is an outrageous allegation. Bishop Martino is one of our finest bishops. His ranking for collections, indulgences and rents from church property is the highest for a bishopric of his size. He has completely turned it around from the performance of his predecessor, not that I knew him, but it is in the records. No, this is a malicious allegation, from some embittered farmer who considers that we have squeezed his rent too much.'

'I see. Well, we wondered if a former choirboy who had been abused might have murdered their abuser. Gino Torelli was a former choirboy who had suffered such abuse. But as Hugh pointed out, the manner of the murders did not match the crime. Why waste time on bales of hay and burning, when Hugh would have cut his balls off?' Aldobrandini jumped up from his chair and paced back and forth.

'Which other suspects have you interviewed?'

'In Florence, we interviewed Andrea Satoro. He has no alibi for Saint Benedict's Day, but a corroborated alibi for Saint Eusabius's Day. It was in Florence that Hugh saw Brother Vitale, and we realised the progress the murders were making towards Rome. There is another suspect who was out of the city, a Mario Tuscani. Hugh stayed behind to interview him, whilst I made best speed for Rome, with Vitale.'

'I see, so there is no clear suspect. Have you any connections to Venice?'

'None, Your Eminence.'

'Sir Anthony, through all my years of hearing confession, I have developed an instinct for when someone is telling the truth, when they are not telling the truth, and when they are hiding something. You are hiding something. I urge you not to play games with me, Sir Anthony. What have you found?'

'Nothing significant, Your Eminence.'

'And what have you uncovered that is insignificant?'

'Gino Torelli visited Venice during one summer vacation.'

'And?'

'Galileo suggested he could stay with Paolo.'

'Now we get to the root of the matter. Has he been back there recently?'

'No. He has a young wife who is expecting their first child. His father died last year, and he is working hard on the farm.'

'Have they been in correspondence?'

'There have been exchanges of letters at Christmas, that is all. I have examined the letters for codes and ciphers, but they are straightforward, with no hidden meaning.'

'You will bring them to me. I will have our cipher office examine them. I think I shall send our chief inquisitor, and his assistants, to question Torelli. They will extract the truth from him.'

'No, I assure you, Gino is innocent. I'm certain of it.'

'If he is, he has nothing to fear. Now if you would be so kind as to fetch the letters, that will be all. Thank you, Sir Anthony, we are most grateful for you service.'

Hugh returned to Rome on Saturday.

'It's good to see you again, Hugh.'

'And it's good to see you too, although you don't quite look yourself. What's happened?'

'I briefed Aldobrandini on our interviews. He's a cunning bastard, he really is. Somehow he squeezed out of me Gino's correspondence with Paolo.'

'It was quite innocent letters you said they were.'

'And so they are, but the bastard says he will send the chief inquisitor and his henchmen to "extract the truth" from Gino.'

'My god! Torture?'

'Of course.'

'Will it work?'

'Have you ever been tortured?'

'I have not.'

'Well I almost was, once.'

'Almost? What do you mean, almost?'

'A fellow who was with me when I was captured in Bordeaux. Our captors tortured him. I heard it all from

117

my cell. The poor sod gave them all they wanted after they chopped only one finger off. They did not need to torture me.'

'Well, if Gino has nothing to hide, he'll be alright then, won't he?'

'I'm not so sure. If that poor sod in Bordeaux hadn't had anything to give them, I don't think they'd have stopped.'

'How do you mean?'

'They have to ask questions. You can't just say "tell us everything", can you? You have to reveal what you're looking for. If they'd asked for names and addresses, he might have invented some. When those proved to be false, he'd have lost another finger. Oh god, you should have heard him, Hugh. He would have accused his neighbours, his friends and his family, rather than lose all his fingers. I can't swear I wouldn't have done the same.'

'Christ! Well, I don't see what we can do about it, to be sure I don't.'

'Neither do I, but I feel so bloody guilty.'

'I think all we can do is track down the real culprit as soon as we can, prove Gino's innocence, and get the cardinal to call his hounds off.'

'I suppose you're right. Did you interview Tuscani?'

'So I did, and the physique for it he has, so he does. He doesn't have an alibi for Abbot Fontana's murder. In fact, he was doing business in Bologna at the time. After his studies, he entered his father's business as a cloth merchant, and has been running it since his father died three years ago. All over the place it takes him. He says he was in Rome on business for a few days on either side of Saint Benedict's Day, so we should be able to check that out. I have the name of the tailor he was supplying. He said he was receiving imported cloth in Livorno three days after Saint Eusebius's Day, but I thought I'd better come straight back here rather than check that out, so I did.'

'Good work, Hugh, I agree. Did he seem to have any motive?'

'That he does not. Galileo was an inspiring tutor, he thought, and believes the Earth rotates around the sun. To be sure, he keeps quiet about it and doesn't want any trouble. He just wants to build up his business, so he does. A wife and a young family he has to support.'

'Did you see them?'

'Yes, it was a touching family scene.'

'That rules him out. What fool would risk their young family losing their breadwinner.'

'Erm, nobody,' Hugh replied under his breath.

'Yes, all right. I suppose I am doing exactly that, thanks to you and the cardinal, but we're here now, and I suppose we are doing something worthwhile. We need to find the actual killer, and save poor Gino.'

'And there is a hefty reward. How are the cardinal's men getting on with the remaining suspects?'

'Well, I think I have scared the bejesus out of the cardinal, as you put it. Perhaps that's why he put so much pressure on me. He's been organising guards equipped with homing pigeons. They're going to Terni, Orte, Viterbo, Fiano Romano, Sutri and Bracciano. If he strikes in any of those places, we should know about it by carrier pigeon within a day, and we can make an educated guess at his next destination.'

'Does it feel like we're closing in on him, does it now?'

'What it feels like is that he's closing in on us, or rather, on the church in Rome. I wouldn't want to be in Pope Paul's shoes, but yes, I think with the homing pigeons we can outwit him. When you're rested, shall we speak to this tailor that Tuscani was supplying?'

'Let's be getting it over with. It's not far, I believe.' Hugh took a scrap of paper from his purse and examined it. 'The tailor's shop is on a street near the Pantheon.'

'You're right, that's not far, we can walk it.' They signed out at the guardhouse of the Quirinal palace and headed towards the Pantheon. The streets were busy with pedestrians, riders on horseback, and a multitude of horse-drawn carts. Both Anthony and Hugh stared at the driver of each passing cart, hoping to recognise one of their suspects. At a small square they had to stop as a drover herded a flock of sheep across the road. To their right, a statue on a tall, red-granite column caught Hugh's eye.

'Who's the statue of?'

'That's Antoninius Pius, a Roman emperor. Marcus Aurelius erected it,' Anthony replied. When the sheep were clear, they continued on their way, and found the tailor's shop just across the road from the Pantheon, which was shrouded by scaffolding. 'Are you renovating it?' Anthony asked a workman who was offloading stone blocks from a cart.

'Building two bell towers,' was the gruff reply. They entered the tailor's shop. Shelves lined the walls, on which were stacked bolts of cloth. The top shelf appeared to be for silk. The middle shelves were for wool, and the lower shelves were for cotton. The silks seemed to be in every colour imaginable. The wools were red, blue, brown and green, and the cotton was predominantly white.

'Can I help you, gentlemen?' the tailor asked, running his eye up and down their apparel. Anthony felt a little uncomfortable. Although his clothes were well tailored, they were designed for working in the vineyard and riding. They were also rather shabby now. Hugh's clothes, although also shabby, were a colourful blend of green, yellow and red wool.

'Would it be Pietro Pirras that you are now?' Hugh asked.

'Yes, perhaps you would like new coats, or would you prefer that I clean and make repairs?'

'We are conducting an investigation for Pope Paul,' Anthony replied. 'Do you buy cloth from a Florentine merchant by the name of Mario Tuscani?'

'I do occasionally. I buy cloth from many suppliers, but Tuscani supplies excellent silks, and has some fine English woollen fabrics. These are some of his woollens. The English wool is the best there is,' he said, walking over to a purple roll of cloth. 'I could make you a fine coat in this, I think it would suit you.'

'Can you tell us when you took deliveries from Tuscani?'

'I'm afraid I can't.'

'Why not?'

'A few weeks ago, my apprentice was taking my

ledgers to my accountant. Some ruffians accosted him on a bridge, and he dropped the ledger into the Tiber. I've been trying to rack my memory to recreate the ledger as best I can, but I fear the tax collectors may think I am trying to defraud them. I'm writing to my customers and suppliers to see if they can provide copies of receipts and invoices. But I haven't got around to writing to Mario yet.'

'Can you remember roughly when you saw him this year?'

'It was the summer, I think, July probably.'

'Can you be more specific?'

'Definitely between mid-June and the end of August.'

'Think man! Was there any specific garment you needed the cloth for? We need to know exactly when you saw him.'

'Well, I used some of it for a robe I made for Cardinal Bellarmine. If you're working for Pope Paul, perhaps you could ask the cardinal when I delivered his robe. It would be very kind of you. Perhaps you could also ask him for a certified copy of my invoice? It would be extremely helpful, when I have to explain things to the tax collector, if it wouldn't be too much trouble?'

'Too much trouble!' Anthony exclaimed as the tailor cowered back against his shelves.

'Come, Anthony, he can't tell us what he doesn't know now, can he?' Hugh said calmly, tugging him by the arm. 'I have the tiredness on me now. We can try Cardinal Bellarmine back at the palace.'

When they got back to the palace, they went to

122

Cardinal Aldobrandini's office.

'Your Eminence, do you know where we can find Cardinal Bellarmine?' Anthony asked.

'This is an interesting development: what do you want to speak to him about?'

'To verify the alibi of one of our suspects, Mario Tuscani. He claims to have been in Rome delivering cloth to a tailor near the Pantheon. Unfortunately, the tailor has lost his ledger, and can't remember exactly when Tuscani delivered the cloth, but he remembers using it for a robe he made for Cardinal Bellarmine. If we can establish when the robe was delivered, the tailor may be able to work out when the cloth he received the cloth, so he can,' Hugh explained.

'Well, you're in luck. Robert is rather fastidious about residing where he is bishop, so you would normally have a five-day ride south to Capua, on the outskirts of Naples. However, because of this trouble with Venice, he has been summoned to Rome. He was with Pope Paul earlier, but you will find him at the Jesuit college of Saint Andrew, just around the corner.'

'Thank you, Your Eminence,' they both replied, and left. In a few minutes, they presented themselves at the porter's lodge, and were taken to Cardinal Bellarmine's room. Robert Bellarmine stood up as Hugh and Anthony were ushered in. He was only a little shorter than Anthony, slim, with black hair and beard and piercing, brown eyes. He was wearing a red robe.

'How can I help you, gentlemen? Please sit down.'

'We are carrying out an investigation for Pope Paul and are trying to verify the alibi of a suspect. Can you tell us if you purchased a new robe recently, from a tailor named Pietro Pirras, who has a shop near the Parthenon?' Anthony asked.

'Yes, the one I am wearing.'

'Can you tell us when he delivered it?'

'I should have the invoice in my papers, let me see,' he said, taking a bundle of papers from a shelf next to his desk and undoing the ribbon that held them together. 'Yes, here it is. He dated the invoice the third of August, the day after Saint Eusebius's Day. How does that help you?'

'The tailor has lost his ledger, but if we tell him when you received the robe, he thinks he can tell us when he received the cloth. That may or may not establish an alibi for the supplier of the cloth.'

'This is all very mysterious. What is it you are investigating?'

'I am afraid we are sworn to secrecy, Your Eminence.'

'Very well. Is that all?'

'Almost, Your Eminence. The tailor would like a copy of the invoice, for the tax authorities, if it is not too much trouble.'

'I shall arrange it, anything else?'

'A small thing, but it may be relevant to our enquiries. Cardinal Aldobrandini said that you would normally be in Capua, but that you were called to Rome because of the troubles with Venice. Why is that?'

'The spokesman for the Venetians is Paolo Sarpi. Whilst we differ on several key theological points, he knows how I detest the abuse of power by many of my fellow cardinals. He trusts me more than the others, and without wishing to appear conceited, only I am his intellectual equal. I take Pope Paul's instructions, but correspond with Sarpi in as effective a way as we can achieve, without force.'

'I see. We have spoken with Paolo Sarpi, and he is a fascinating man. May I ask what abuses of power you refer to, amongst your fellow cardinals, that is?'

'Is it relevant to your enquiry?'

'It may be.'

'Well, since you have met Sarpi, did you know that six years ago they recommended him for the bishopric of Caorle?'

'No.'

'Well, our papal nuncio in Venice told Pope Clement that Sarpi denied the immortality of the soul and corresponded with heretics. The bishopric went to a cousin of the papal nuncio instead. I think it was rather a flimsy argument to deny Brother Sarpi the bishopric, but the nuncio achieved his aim. To me, it seemed to be an abuse of power. But he was just one amongst many. Several cardinals have taken multiple bishoprics in such far distant places that they cannot possibly visit all of their bishoprics in a lifetime.'

'Why do they then?'

'For the money. It is immaterial to me, but for someone like Pietro, Aldobrandini that is, not my tailor, his art collection and his palaces seem to bring him great joy.'

'I didn't know he had his own palace. He appears to live in the Quirinal Palace.'

'He is restoring his recently acquired Palazzo Doria,

which is on the Via del Corso, and in the meantime, he lives in the Quirinal. Please don't ask me which is the largest, but it is immense. He has only just completed rebuilding the villa which his uncle, Pope Clement, gave him.'

'Is that also in Rome?' Anthony asked.

'Why would he need two palaces in Rome? No, that is in Frascati.'

'Good heavens, my vineyard is close to Frascati. We are virtually neighbours.'

'I doubt you will see him there very often; it is for impressing people he wants something from.'

'This trouble with Sarpi, so it is about his denying the immortality of the soul, is it?' Anthony enquired.

'Anthony, Your Eminence, it's dog tired I am. If you would excuse me, I will go back to your tailor and check with him what date he received the cloth. I'll see you back at the Quirinal, Anthony,' Hugh said as he got up and left.

'Where were we? Ah yes, is the problem with Sarpi about him denying the immortality of the soul? No, not really, it is about power and money. His holiness has tried to extend the papal prerogative and the Venetians have tried to restrict it.'

'Your Eminence, our conversation with Sarpi troubled me. I think Hugh and I both liked him, yet his argument about the mortality of the soul shook everything I have believed in. What do you believe?'

'I am a Thomist, that is I follow the philosophy of Thomas Aquinas. He was a man of immense intellect, who drew upon the philosophies of Aristotle and the

Spanish moor, Averroës. Thomas tried to reconcile faith and reason.'

'Why, and in what way?' Anthony enquired.

'Man has an inquisitive mind, and sometimes a powerful intellect. The church is built on faith, and asserts that the holy scriptures, all of them, are the divine revelation of truth from God. If man could disprove some aspect of the holy scriptures, then that assertion casts doubt on the entire edifice of faith. This is the great concern surrounding Galileo. He is an impressively intelligent man, and he reasons that the Earth orbits the sun, whilst we have interpreted scripture to say otherwise.'

'I see, Galileo is not infallible, though. His theory that the moon has nothing to do with tides, I know to be incorrect.'

'Really, Sir Anthony?'

'Oh yes. If you sail in the waters around the British Isles, as I have, then it is starkly obvious that the moon has a very significant effect on tides. But how did Thomas reconcile reason with faith?'

'By using reason to prove the existence of God. In his work, Quinque Viae, he set out five ways to prove the existence of God. There are similarities, so I will outline just two. The first mover argument is that everything that moves has been caused to move. Since the first thing that moved had to be caused to move, that cause must be God. The proof of degrees is that in nature we find different degrees of things, like heat, goodness, nobility, truth, etc. Therefore, there must exist something that is the greatest degree of all things, and in consequence the greatest being, God.'

'The church must have been very grateful for Thomas' work. But the church is the Christian church, and I don't recall Jesus Christ insisting that the sun orbits the Earth. Wouldn't it be easier for the church to place more emphasis on the gospels than the books of the Old Testament?'

'You are a rather inquisitive man yourself, Sir Anthony. The assertion of the infallibility of the scriptures is long standing, and difficult to back away from. It would also be inconvenient to do so. Some would assert, for instance, that there is nothing in Christ's teaching that supports the use of corporal punishment or torture. There are many supportive texts in the Old Testament, and indeed the book of Revelation, that condone physical and mental punishment and torture. The work of the Inquisition would be called into question, were it not for the scriptures other than the gospels. As to the church being grateful for Thomas's work, the answer is yes and no. Thomas was accused, amongst other things, of elevating reason above faith, and failing to make clear the immortality of the soul. He was excommunicated a few years after his death, then made a saint five years later. So getting back to the immortality of the soul, if it is a comfort to you, perhaps the soul has two parts. There is the part that we believe is who we are, and there is the part that is divine and immortal.'

'That does sound rather similar to Sarpi's idea. He said that God would absorb him.'

'He is an eminent scholar. Consider also the resurrection of our saviour, Jesus Christ.'

'What do you mean?'

'His body was required for him to appear to the disciples. The women found the body of Jesus missing from the tomb. It had to be the resurrected mortal Jesus, in order to appear as himself. If there were a ghostly Jesus that could appear to the disciples, some part of the soul that has an individual identity, why was it necessary that his mortal body be brought back to life, in order for him to appear before his disciples?'

'Why then, is this philosophy not more widely known?'

'It is amongst those who can understand it. The ordinary people need more comfort in their inevitable grief. They also need law and order. If the fires of damnation were to lose their power of persuasion, then law and order might suffer.'

'I see,' Anthony said, as there was a knock at the door.

'Come in!' Bellarmine called. The door opened and Guardsman Pfyffer entered.

'Excuse me, Your Eminence, but Cardinal Aldobrandini sent me to fetch Sir Anthony and Earl O'Neill. He said that a pigeon has arrived.'

'I'll come at once. Hugh has gone to check an alibi with the cardinal's tailor. He'll join us there. Excuse me, Your Eminence. You have given me a lot to think about.'

Hugh rushed back to the Pantheon. He entered the shop of the tailor, Pietro Pirras.

'You dated your invoice the third of August. Can you tell from that when you received the cloth from Tuscani?'

'Oh yes. It was a rush job, and Tuscani's cloth was

holding me up. It took me three long days to complete it, and I ran round to the cardinal with the finished robes on the third. I received the cloth just before I shut up the shop, so that would have been the thirty-first of July.'

'So was it definitely Tuscani who delivered it, not a messenger?'

'Yes, it was Tuscani.'

Hugh thought for a few seconds. Rome to Ferrara is two hundred and sixty miles. He'll not be doing that in two days. But he could have reached Livorno in five days, so he could. 'Thank you, Signor Pirras.'

Anthony and Guardsman Pfyffer bumped into Hugh as they entered the Quirinal Palace.

'It can't have been Tuscani, Anthony. His alibi is solid, so it is.' They walked briskly to Cardinal Aldobrandini's study.

'We came as quickly as we could, Your Eminence. What has happened?' Anthony asked, breathing hard.

'It is curious. Cardinal Pinelli's tailor has been killed, in the same fashion as the clerical victims. They are bringing Cardinal Pinelli here. He should be here by the morning. He would have been either in Ostia, which is about seventeen miles to the east, or Velletri, twenty-four miles to the south. You look exhausted, Earl O'Neill. I suggest you both get some rest and I shall call for you when Cardinal Pinelli arrives.'

'We shall, so we will, thank you, Your Eminence,' Hugh said.

'You should close the palace to everyone, other than Cardinal Pinelli and his escort, Your Eminence. The murderer will be ahead of them, so may already be in Rome,' Anthony added.

'You're right. Guardsman Pfyffer, convey that instruction to the guardroom.'

Anthony lay on his bed, listening enviously to Hugh snoring in the adjoining room. He thought through each of the suspects they had interviewed, none of whom seemed to have an obvious motive. This killer had to be driven by an intense rage, directed at the church and concerning heliocentricity in some way. He is also clever, and very strong, or has an accomplice. He can pick locks, so has learnt that from a locksmith or another criminal. What happens when you die? Sarpi and Bellarmine are both intelligent, and souls are their stock in trade, yet they don't seem to believe in life after death. Paolo seemed to make the most sense. To be absorbed by God, become a part of God again, immortal, invisible, indivisible perhaps. Maybe he should ask Cardinal Bellarmine what he thinks of the theory about credit and debit. That in the beginning there was nothing, and that God and satan were opposites that cancelled each other out, like a debit and credit. Then they split apart, creating heaven and hell, and everything in between. Then again, perhaps he shouldn't. They might burn him as a heretic. His mind drifted back to his father, and the day that he had taken him to Gray's Inn, how he had wandered the streets of London while his father was in a meeting, and how he had seen the Islington martyrs burnt at the stake. He was listening to their screams, smelling their burning flesh and wondering what the banging noise was when he awoke with a start, sweat streaming down his face, and got up to open the door.

'The cardinal wants to see you, sir,' Guardsman Pfyffer announced.

'What time is it?'

'Eight o'clock in the morning, Sir Anthony. Cardinal Pinelli arrived last night. He is rested and ready to answer questions. Earl O'Neill is up and ready to go.'

'Very well, just give me a second.' Anthony pulled on his breeches and his doublet, then washed his face in the bowl of water on the chest of drawers by the window. He ran his fingers through his hair. 'Let's go then, lead on.'

Cardinal Aldobrandini was standing talking to another man of average height, with hollow cheeks and high eyebrows which sloped towards a long, roman-nose. Anthony estimated his age as mid to late sixties. Cardinal Aldobrandini ushered them to a large table at the far end of the room from his desk, where there were chairs for them all, with six to spare.

'Domenico, these gentlemen are helping us with an investigation which concerns the recent event in Ostia. This is Sir Anthony Standen, and this is Earl O'Neill of Tyrone. Please tell us what happened, Domenico. Leave no detail out.'

'Well Pietro, it was yesterday evening, Saint Januarius Day. I was in my study in Santa Aurea, working on my sermon for today. My tailor, Marco Danielli, arrived at about seven o'clock with a new robe for a fitting that we had arranged. He had hardly unwrapped the robe when I was called away to give the last rites to a parishioner, when—'

'Why you? Surely another priest could have attended him?' Cardinal Aldobrandini asked.

'The plague has been quite bad this year. Everyone else was already out administering the last rites.'

'I see, yes, of course, carry on.'

'So I asked Danielli to wait and said I'd be back as soon as I could. I wanted to wear the new robes on Sunday, you see, and if there were any alterations required, I wanted them done that evening. I got back about two hours later and Danielli seemed to have vanished, and so had my robe. Then I smelt smoke and went to investigate. I unlocked the door to the Basilica and there was a fearsome blaze in the apse. As I approached it to see what was happening, the door slammed shut behind me. I looked around, but there was nobody there. In the fire, I could just discern the face of Danielli. Oh, sweet Jesus, the contortions in his face, the smell...' Pinelli held his face in his hands, and sobbed. 'He was wearing my new robes.'

'Why would he have been wearing your robes?' Anthony asked.

'He was almost exactly my height and build. He had remarked on it when I first employed his services. I can only imagine he thought he'd try them on himself and see how they fitted.'

'So the murderer would have mistaken him for you.'

'Yes, I suppose so. Oh my god, yes. But why? Who would want to kill me?'

'Domenico, there have been a series of similar murders, all committed on saints' days with priests as the victims. They have been leading from Venice towards Rome, and you are the first cardinal to be targeted. We think the motive has something to do with the heretical belief that the sun is at the centre of the universe. Can you think of anyone who might be responsible?' Cardinal Aldobrandini asked.

'No, but, perhaps, no it can't be.'

'Who, Domenico? We have no time to waste.'

'Can he have risen from hell? No surely not.'

'Who, man? Tell us!'

'Bruno, Giordano Bruno. I sat on the inquisition. Eight years it took before he was burnt at the stake, here in Rome, in the Campo de Fiori.'

'And was he a believer in heliocentricity?' Anthony asked.

'Well, yes, but we weren't interested in that very much, as I recall. You should ask Robert Bellarmine, he was the chief inquisitor. Pope Paul was also an inquisitor, but of course he wasn't the pope then.'

'His holiness may be a target too. This devil has to be stopped, but how?' Cardinal Aldobrandini exclaimed.

'Cardinal Pinelli, when was it that Giordano Bruno was burnt?' Anthony asked.

'I remember distinctly, because of the irony, it was Ash Wednesday you see. Oh don't think unkindly of me, sir,' Pinelli exclaimed as he saw the suppressed rage in Anthony's eyes.

'What year?' Anthony asked.

'1600, sir.'

'And what age was he?'

'I can't say exactly, he looked so much older by the

end of the trial you see, but perhaps he was in his mid-forties when I first saw him. You should ask Robert, he will know where the records of the trial are kept in the papal library.'

'Did he have any family who might want to avenge him?'

'Oh, sir, I beg you, I don't remember. I have tried to expunge it from my mind. Such blasphemies uttered by such a gentle intelligent soul.'

'Yes, Domenico, we will speak with Robert,' Cardinal Aldobrandini said, getting up and walking to the door. He opened it. 'Guardsman Pfyffer, please fetch Cardinal Bellarmine.'

'At once, Your Eminence.'

Cardinal Aldobrandini crossed to a cabinet and took out five, stemmed wine glasses and a decanter of wine. He poured the wine and gave the first glass to Pinelli, then Anthony, Hugh, one for himself and one for Bellarmine when he arrived.

'You have had a terrible ordeal, Domenico, this will calm you. Please excuse Sir Anthony's manner, but he has been very helpful to us, and is our best hope of catching this fiend. You said you heard a door slam behind you as you approached the fire. Did you hear the lock turned?'

'I don't think so. Perhaps I should have checked the lock, but I wasn't thinking. The roar of the flames was quite loud.'

'Did you hear any footsteps?' Aldobrandini asked while Pinelli took a large gulp of wine.

'I don't know, I may have done, I was looking into poor Danielli's eyes.'

'Please think, Domenico, did you hear one man's footsteps or two?'

'I don't know, Pietro,' Pinelli sobbed. 'I dont know if I heard any footsteps, let alone one man's or two. Ask Robert.'

'We will, Domenico, but he wasn't there, was he? You are the first actual witness we have had.' Before Aldobrandini could go on, the door opened and Cardinal Bellarmine came in. 'Ah Robert, thank you for joining us. Please sit down. I have poured you a glass. You have already met Sir Anthony and Earl Hugh.'

'Yes. Is this about the secret matter that concerned my tailor?' asked Bellarmine as he sat down.

'Your tailor too!' exclaimed Pinelli.

'It's not about tailors. Yes, I'm sorry about the secrecy, Robert. Sir Anthony and Earl Hugh have been investigating a mysterious sequence of murders. We know of four murders and there may be others, news of which hasn't reached us yet. The trail leads from Venice to Rome. In the first three a priest was burnt in his church on a saint's day. The body was surrounded by a ring of earth. Sir Anthony and Hugh think this is a reference to the heresy of heliocentricity, and they may be right. We think Domenico was the target of the most recent attack, but his tailor was trying on his new robes while Domenico went to a dying parishioner, and the tailor was killed instead. Domenico thinks it may have something to do with Giordano Bruno. You were the chief inquisitor we believe.'

'Yes, that's correct, Pietro. How can I help?'

'May I, Your Eminence?' Anthony asked.

Aldobrandini nodded. 'We need to establish who may be trying to avenge Bruno. He was a proponent of heliocentricity we believe?'

'Yes he was.'

'And was that the crime for which he was burnt?'

'That was only a minor matter. In fact, if I remember rightly, we didn't bring it up, he did. The trial was eight years of him trying to persuade us of his theories, and us demonstrating to him how wrong he was, through the holy scriptures. He had many dangerous beliefs, that knowledge is the path to salvation, rather than faith for example. I would have to consult the records to be sure, but I think the charges were: denial of eternal damnation; denial of the Holy Trinity; denial of the divinity of Christ; denial of the virginity of Mary; and denial of transubstantiation. It's the liberal intellectuals who claim we convicted him for his Copernican ideas.'

'Is it possible that he has relatives, or close friends, who could be behind these murders?' Anthony enquired.

'I don't recollect mention of any siblings.'

'Did he have any children?'

'I doubt it, he was homosexual.'

'Are you sure he wasn't bi-sexual, Robert? I seem to recollect the testimony of some aggrieved husbands,' Pinelli added.

'Possibly, but either way it wasn't why he was burnt. It was simply the legality to permit it. It was our part of a deal with Spain.'

'Can you explain that, please?' Anthony asked.

'Certainly, but give me a few minutes to retrieve my notes from the library. The records of the inquisition fill several volumes, but I kept a notebook as a summary to aid my memory, which isn't as good as his was.' Cardinal Aldobrandini refreshed the wine glasses as they waited for Bellarmine to return. 'Yes, this is the page.' Bellarmine sat down again. 'When Bruno got to Paris in 1581, he became quite successful with his memory demonstrations. He had mastered something he called mnemonics. He used elaborate songs, rhymes and mental pictures to trigger memories of facts. He came to the attention of the French court and King Henry III. At first Henry accused him of sorcery, but Bruno convinced him of the power of mnemonics, from which point Bruno received Henry's patronage. The chasm and warring between Protestants and Catholics disturbed Bruno, and he sought to reconcile the heretics with the one true church. He travelled to London with a letter of recommendation from King Henry, and worked with the French ambassador there, a Michel de Castelnau, if I remember correctly. Bruno set to work infiltrating the English court and the liberal intellectuals. His aim was an alliance between England and France. Unfortunately for him, Spain was building an armada to defeat the English navy, which had been a thorn in Spain's side. The very last thing Spain wanted was England and France to be allies, and control both sides of the English Channel. Spain was then the greatest supporter of the papacy and wanted Bruno dead.'

'How long was Bruno in England?' Anthony enquired.

'Let me see,' Bellarmine replied running his index finger down the page of his notebook and flicking a few pages. 'He was in London from April 1583 until October

1585, when a mob of rioters attacked the French embassy. Bruno fled via France to Germany, then to Venice and Padua, where he taught for a while. There he applied for the chair in mathematics, but it went to Galileo instead.'

'Venice again. I knew they were behind this,' mused Aldobrandini. 'Did he know Paolo Sarpi?'

'I don't know, he may have done,' Bellarmine replied, flicking through his notebook.

'So he was in London for around two and a half years,' Anthony said, running his fingers through his beard.

'Yes, he wrote and published six books while he was there. Ah, here is my list, they were: Italian Dialogues, On Cause, Principle and Unity; On the Infinite, Universe and Worlds; The Expulsion of the Triumphant Beast; On the Heroic Frenzies; and The Supper of Ashes.'

'The Supper of Ashes, that rings a bell now, so it does,' Hugh remarked. 'That's right, it was a book on Sarpi's book shelf. Do you remember, Anthony, you asked him about it?'

'Yes that's right, I asked him if it was about burning people.'

'There, we have our evidence. Sarpi is behind this,' Aldobrandini said smiling.

'No, I don't think so. What was the name of the English painter, Hugh?'

'Mark Brown, I think.'

'Bruno, brown, bruno is one of the Italian words for brown. Didn't he say that his father was a French diplomat? I'm sure he did. He must have learnt about his father when he was studying in Padua, and found out how he was killed.'

'Brown didn't seem to have the strength to haul a body to a fire.'

'He may have an accomplice. Anyway, my daughter can throw a man twice her weight to the ground. You can achieve a lot with technique.'

'And rage,' Hugh added.

'I'm sure Mark Brown is our man,' Anthony exclaimed.

'Well, I still think Sarpi is behind this. But you confirmed Sarpi's alibis, so this Mark Brown may be an agent for Sarpi. Did Brown have an alibi?' Aldobrandini asked.

'Not really. He said he was confined to bed with a fever, but he could have been faking it. He would have had to travel fast to commit the murder on Saint Benedict's Day, since the apothecary saw him at nine o'clock that morning. But it's what, about thirteen miles from Padua to Monselice, he could have done it. He didn't have an alibi at all for the murder in Ferrara.'

'Perhaps Sarpi convinced him that Bruno was his father and gave him the idea of revenge. Either way he is heading this way and Robert may be his intended ultimate victim, or worse still, Pope Paul, sorry Robert. Sir Anthony, you and Earl Hugh are the only ones here who know what Brown looks like.'

'I could try to make a sketch of him, if you would lend me a page from your notebook, and a pen and ink.' Bellarmine tore out a page from his notebook and Aldobrandini passed his writing slope with ink wells and quills to Anthony. Anthony began sketching. 'I suggest you all, and Pope Paul, confine yourselves to the palace until we find him. Ensure that none of you is alone at any point. Hugh and I will take Sergeant Hennard and Guardsman Pfyffer and start patrolling the surrounding area. If we don't catch him, he could bide his time and strike again when your guard is down.'

'Yes, and you wouldn't get your reward,' Aldobrandini added, as Anthony continued sketching, and Hugh clenched his fists under the table. Bellarmine stood up and walked around to Anthony, peering over his shoulder at the emerging likeness of Mark Brown.

'You are a fine draughtsman, Sir Anthony. I dabble, but you have the finer hand. I made several sketches of Bruno over the years. Let me see.' He flicked through his notebook. 'Here is an early sketch.' He glanced from his own sketch to Anthony's and back again. In a few more pen strokes, Anthony was satisfied with his sketch. 'Sir Anthony, that is impressive. I could not possibly draw a face from memory.'

'It is a talent I discovered on a hillside outside A Coruña, when I made a perfect sketch from memory.'

'May I?' Bellarmine asked, reaching for Anthony's sketch. Anthony handed it to him and Bellarmine walked around to Aldobrandini. He placed Anthony's sketch on the table and his notebook open at his own sketch of Bruno. 'Pietro, I have no doubt that Brown is Bruno's son. Look at the likeness.'

'It's true. The evil in Sarpi has turned Brown to avenge his father. I wonder how long it took him, showing him the books his father had written, recounting the trial and the execution.'

'Can we please focus on Brown? Hugh, let's collect Hennard and Pfyffer, and get started,' Anthony said.

'Yes, I accept that is the top priority. I will have an artist make some copies of your sketch and distribute them amongst the palace guard.' Aldobrandini agreed.

CHAPTER EIGHT

Anthony, Hugh, Sergeant Hennard and Guardsman Pfyffer left the Quirinal Palace by the gatehouse at the south-eastern corner of the palace, onto the Via del Quirinale. 'My suggestion, Hugh, is that we patrol the perimeter in opposite directions. I'll take Sergeant Hennard, and you take Guardsman Pfyffer. That way we'll cover more ground, and I'm sure either of us will recognise him.'

'That makes sense to me, Anthony, so it does. What is it we do when we spot him?'

'Follow him. We need evidence.'

'What sort of evidence? If he's driving a cart with bales of straw and a cask of brandy, is that enough?'

'I daresay that would satisfy Cardinal Aldobrandini. He'd torture a confession out of him which would implicate Paolo Sarpi. How do you feel? I want more evidence before I have his blood on my conscience. We must catch him in the act.'

'There we go now. That will be after dark, I imagine, if he carries on as he has so far. It would be safest for him. Will we recognise him in the dark?'

'Probably not. We'll have to hope that we spot him before it gets dark and then follow him. I suppose he'll either go to where he will attack his next victim, or where he will prepare the murder scene.'

'Anthony, if it's Cardinal Bellarmine he's after, he may be on his way to where he should be, in Capua, near Naples.'

'Good point. If so, he'll be on a fool's errand. But if he's going after Pope Paul, then he'll try to pick a lock and get into the palace. With most of the palace guard still on the lookout for him to the north of Rome, there are several gates into the gardens that are unguarded. He may try one of those. Let's start our patrols. Sergeant Hennard and I will head off north east up the Via del Quirinale, you and Pfyffer head north west and circle around on the Via del Giardini.' They set off. After ten minutes, they met again at the north corner of the wall around the extensive gardens. 'Did you see anything, Hugh?'

'We didn't. We gave each garden gate a rattle as we passed. They're all securely locked.'

'Let's carry on then,' said Anthony. He and Sergeant Hennard continued their patrol until they reached a junction with the Via della Panetteria. They were just about to turn left when they heard the rumbling of a cart's wheels behind them. As it passed, Anthony looked at the driver. He let it pass, then grabbed Hennard's sleeve. 'I think that's him,' Anthony whispered.

'Are you sure, sir?'

'I think so. Let's get after him.' Anthony and Sergeant Hennard had to hurry to keep up with the cart. It continued past the junction with the Via del Giardini, at which point they would have turned left to continue their patrol. They had to break into a jog to keep it in sight, but after about two hundred yards, it slowed and turned left into a side street. Anthony and Hennard continued to the corner with the side street and stopped. Anthony peered around the corner. Then he put his finger to his lips, and whispered into Hennard's ear. 'He's climbed down and is opening a stable door.' They waited silently and heard the slight crack of the reins and the rumble of the wheels, followed by the creak of the stable door being closed. Anthony took another look. 'He's inside.'

'What do we do now, sir?'

'I'll stay here. You sneak around the stable building and see if there are any other doors he can exit from. Then come back here.' Hennard nodded and set off, keeping low and treading as quietly as he could. Anthony continued to look up and down the street, and around the corner at the stable door. A few minutes later, Hennard rejoined him.

'There are no other exits, sir. We've got him pinned down. What do we do next?'

'It's getting dark. He may make his move soon. I'll stay here and keep watch. You intercept Hugh and Guardsman Pfyffer and bring them here. Then we'll all follow him, in the shadows, and see what he's up to. You and Pfyffer should hang back a bit, in case he makes out your uniforms, or sees your weapons. Hugh and I will alternate being in the lead. We won't need to get too close. We're unlikely to lose him with those rumbling wheels.'

'I'd be happier if I stayed and kept watch, sir, and you went to fetch the others.'

'You're wasting time, sergeant. I've shown you I can look after myself, and I've been trained in covert surveillance. Get going!' Sergeant Hennard set off at a brisk pace back towards the junction with the Via del Giardini. As it continued to darken, Anthony crept around the corner. He pressed himself against the wall, in the shadows, and inched his way towards the stable door. Every few feet, he stopped and listened. All he could hear was the occasional rumble of carts from the street behind him. When he got to the door, he peered through a crack between the door frame and the door. There was the dim glow of an oil lamp inside, and he could see Brown swinging a bale of straw up onto the cart. He didn't seem to have any accomplice, and he was stronger than he looked. Brown moved out of the limited range of vision the crack afforded Anthony, and he shuffled to one side, trying to see more. He thought he could see Brown coming back to the cart, carrying a small cask. He heard a slight inhalation of breath behind him and spun around, then everything went black.

The first thing Anthony sensed was an aroma and a burning sensation in his throat. He thought it was vanilla. Yes, he was sure he detected vanilla, certainly oak, and perhaps a hint of liquorice and peach, too. Brandy, he concluded. He tried to remember where he was. He had been outside a stable and watching someone lift a cask.

He struggled to think clearly. His head was throbbing. As he opened his eyes, he discerned a blurred image, which cleared slowly and became God. Other images came into focus, and he realised he was looking at a fresco on the ceiling of a church. He tried to get up but couldn't move his arms or legs. He turned his head to the left and saw that his wrist had been tied. The rope ran over the side of a wooden board and down beyond his vision. He lifted his head as far as he could. His ankle appeared to be secured in the same way. He turned his head to the right, and the same was true of his right wrist and ankle. There was an oil lamp burning on the floor about five yards away. There was straw strewn all over the floor. A hooded figure appeared.

'Good evening, Sir Anthony. I hadn't expected to see you again so soon.' Anthony squirmed and tried to move his wrists and ankles to loosen the bonds. 'There is no point. That might have worked, but I discovered that placing a wooden board on top of the straw bales provides a much more secure lashing point. There is too much give in the straw itself. If you have any last prayers to say, I suggest you get on with them.'

'Mark Brown, I was watching you through the stable door. Who hit me?'

'Yes, may I introduce you to the hero of the hour, Rotilio Orlandini. Take a bow, Rotilio.' A second figure in a black, hooded-cloak stepped up beside Brown. He was taller and broader. He bowed.

'Where are we?'

'We are in the chapel of Our Lady of Trivio,' Brown replied.

'Are you going to burn me? I'm not a priest.'

'Of course I am, you're working for them.'

'Yes, but only for money. I'm becoming rather convinced that the Earth does orbit the sun. Scientific reasoning seems more convincing than the interpretation of an obscure verse in Genesis. Are you sure you wouldn't rather burn a priest?'

'Well, I was intending to see if I could catch a cardinal this time. I was going to drive around the area near the Quirinal Palace and the Jesuit college. If I couldn't get a cardinal, then any priest would have served my purpose. I already had this chapel earmarked for the fire. Then you turned up instead. You may not be a priest, but you have taken sides with satan, against my crusade for truth and justice. Therefore, you must face the consequences.'

'Don't I deserve a fair trial? Your father's trial lasted eight years.'

'What do you know of my father?'

'I know he was a good, intelligent man, and that his death was a travesty. Where did you learn to pick locks?'

'My step-father was a locksmith.'

'We knew you lied about him being an innkeeper. How did you recruit Rotilio?'

'He came across me, as I was painting in Padua one day, and asked me if I would paint his portrait. Roti has a distinctive face, not handsome, but I thought capturing those sunken eye sockets without losing the depth in the eyes themselves, would be a challenge. We got talking and found that we had a common hatred of the church. He was a defrocked priest, with an interest in money. I told him I could open doors for him,' Brown laughed. 'With my interest in art, I knew what we could steal and where to find it. We both had ideas of who we could sell it to. It has been a successful partnership.'

'Where did you learn about your father?'

'My mother told me as much as she knew; that his name was Giordano Bruno, a French diplomat but born in Nola, near Naples. She said he was a writer. When I was old enough, and had acquired enough money to travel, I went to Italy and enrolled at the University of Padua. I asked my tutor, Galileo Galilei, if he had heard of my father, and I was astonished to hear that he had also taught briefly at Padua. I then started reading his books and asking people what had happened to him. The church burnt my father because he was a man of science; and they placed more importance on an obscure verse in the bible. Anyway, as much as I find you pleasant company, we can't hang around all night. Have you made your peace? We must get on. Roti, light the taper and pass it to me, please.'

'You know that they did not murder him because of his belief in heliocentricity, don't you?'

'Of course he was. What do you know? He championed science against blind faith.'

'Yes, and the matter of heliocentricity was only raised by your father at his trial. The inquisitors weren't interested in it.'

'You lie! How could you know?'

'It's true, haven't you read the records of his trial?'

'How could I? They are in the papal records?'

'Your father was killed as part of an agreement with King Philip of Spain. Your father was trying to negotiate a treaty between France and England. That was why he was in England. Spain feared that if both sides of the English Channel were denied to them, their plans for an armada might fail. They made a treaty with the pope that put a price on your father's head. It took some years for him to fall into the pope's hands, but he could eventually repay his debt.'

'How could you know all this?'

'Firstly, because I was working for Francis Walsingham to defeat the Armada, and secondly because the head of your father's inquisition told me so.'

'Who is he? Tell me!' Brown screamed. Anthony thought he heard a key turning in a lock behind him.

'Yes, I will tell you, if you wait a moment,' Anthony said, raising his voice, 'it was Cardinal Bell —' he saw a red and grey, round hole appear in Brown's forehead. His hood flew backwards, followed by fragments of bone and brain. Rotilio retreated into the shadows. Footsteps pounded towards him.

'Is it all right you are, Anthony?' Hugh asked.

'Barely, cut me free would you.' Hugh cut his bonds and held Anthony's arm as he climbed down from the pyre. 'Thank God you found me. What happened?'

'Unfortunately, Sergeant Hennard didn't bump into us until the far end of the palace grounds, so he didn't. It took us a while to run back to the stable. When we got there, empty it was. I asked Hennard where the nearest church was, and this is it. Fortunately, he knew where the priest lives, and we got the key. You owe your life to your ability to string a story out, a man after my own heart.' Sergeant Hennard and Guardsman Pfyffer appeared from the shadows, holding Rotilio Orlandini between them. Hennard picked up the rope that had bound Anthony and used it to bind Orlandini's wrists. He then used a length to tie his ankles and prevent him from making a run for it.

'Thank you, Sergeant Hennard, I owe you my life.'

'Thank Guardsman Pfyffer, sir. I told you he was a crackshot. You don't look too steady on your feet, if you don't mind me saying so, sir. It looks like you've had a nasty crack on the back of your head.'

'Yes, but I have a thick skull. I've had much worse, I assure you.'

'All the same, their horse and cart must be around the back somewhere. Pfyffer, have a look out the back for the horse and cart and bring it around to the front. We'll use it to take Brown's body back to the palace and give Sir Anthony a lift back.'

'Thank you, my legs are a bit shaky,' Anthony turned to Hugh. 'Thank God this is finally over, Hugh.'

'Amen to that.'

It was not yet dawn when they got back to the Quirinal palace. Guardsman Pfyffer took Orlandini to the dungeons and Anthony, Hugh, and Sergeant Hennard went to Cardinal Aldobrandini's office.

'Come in!' Aldobrandini called out as Sergeant Hennard knocked on the door. 'Goodness, you look awful, Sir Anthony. What happened?'

'We caught him, Your Eminence, red handed,' Anthony replied. 'The only trouble was, it was me that was about to become the next victim. I spotted him on his cart, so Sergeant Hennard and I followed him to a stable building. I sent Sergeant Hennard to fetch the others, whilst I kept watch on the stable. Unfortunately, his accomplice, a defrocked priest by the name of Rotilio Orlandini, crept up on me silently and whacked me on the head. When I woke up, they had tied me down on bales of straw soaked in brandy.'

'However did you escape?' Aldobrandini asked, and Hugh answered.

'When we got to the stable, empty, so it was. I asked Sergeant Hennard where the nearest church was. He took us to Our Lady of Trivio and got the key from the priest. We unlocked the door as silently as we could. Anthony was shouting, so he was, quite loudly at that point, which helped us enter unheard. Guardsman Pfyffer put a rifle shot straight through Brown's forehead, burning taper in his hand. The finest piece of shooting I've ever seen, so it was.'

'You are to be commended, Guardsman Pfyffer, and you too, sergeant. Where is this Orlandini now?'

'He's in the dungeons, Your Eminence,' Sergeant Hennard replied.

'Excellent, and Brown is dead by the sound of it.'

'Yes, Your Eminence, all but half his brain is in his cart, in the courtyard.'

'Well, it saves us the time and expense of a trial.'

'Clearly, Your Eminence, Gino Torelli had nothing to do with it. I trust you will send a messenger to call off the inquisitor now,' Anthony asked.

'Perhaps, but he may have something to connect Sarpi with Brown.'

'Sarpi has nothing whatsoever to do with this, either.

Brown discovered that his father had been burnt, by the church, for his heliocentric ideas, or so he believed. I'm certain that over time it drove him insane, and he decided to avenge his father. You know, Brown I can understand in a way, he was avenging his father. But Orlandini killed innocent priests for money. What kind of monster is that? He can surely have no regard for his immortal soul. I take it he will be tried and executed?'

'Yes, killing for money. You are right, Sir Anthony,' Aldobrandini answered, stoking his beard.

'Talking of money, I wonder if we could be taking our rewards off your hands now?' Hugh enquired. 'I'm sure Anthony is keen to get back to his family, so he is.'

'Yes, of course, but we don't keep those sums of money in the palace. Also, I'm quite sure that His Holiness will wish to reward you both personally. In fact, there is a papal consistory on Wednesday, that is a meeting of all the cardinals in Rome. Yes, that is ideal. His Holiness will sing all your praises and present your rewards. It will turn what looked like a rather dull agenda into a grand thanksgiving for your god-given powers of reason and deduction. You need to rest before travelling, I suggest, Sir Anthony. But whether you stay here or return home, you and Earl Hugh must be here at noon on Wednesday for the presentation of your rewards. I hope that you don't mind the slight delay. After all, I said it would be over in two months, and you've done it in only one.'

Anthony could smell his burning flesh and hear the crackle of the flames devouring him. He could see

Brown's eyes glimmering in the firelight. He struggled to break free of his bonds. When would it end? He sat bolt upright in bed; his shirt soaked in sweat. He decided he wouldn't get much sleep now, so he washed his face in the bowl of water on the chest of drawers and put his clothes on. He went for a walk through the palace corridors. As he turned a corner, he saw Sergeant Hennard.

'Hello, sergeant. I couldn't sleep.'

'I'm not surprised, sir, after your narrow escape.'

'What are you doing, sergeant? Isn't this the pope's suite?'

'Yes, sir,' Hennard said, lowering his voice. 'I can't quite fathom it. I was asked to bring Orlandini up from the dungeons. He's in there now with His Holiness and Cardinal Aldobrandini.'

'Whatever for? I hope he's securely shackled.'

'Oh yes, sir, he's in chains all right, but they told me to wait outside.'

'Well, I suppose they know best. Good night to you, sergeant. And thank you again.' Anthony continued his walk down the corridor but silently counting his paces. At thirty paces, he came to a staircase. He climbed to the floor above and paced out thirty paces back in the direction he had come. There was a door. He tried the handle, but it was locked. He took his set of lock picks from his pocket and had the door unlocked in a few seconds. The room was empty, and he walked swiftly over to the fireplace. He could hear voices from the room below.

'We will burn you, you know, unless you help us.'

'What do you want of me?'

'There is a Venetian that is causing us some difficulty. We would like you to kill him for us.'

'What's it worth?'

'You impudent dog. We will spare your life, isn't that enough?'

'You're not very smart for a pope, are you? As soon as I'm out of Rome, I'm a free man. Why would I put myself at risk, if there's no reward in it?'

'He has a point, Your Holiness. Can I suggest we offer him, say, four thousand crowns, half now and half when the job is complete.'

'What is to stop the scoundrel absconding with the two thousand crowns?'

'That's right, I might just do that,' Orlandini chuckled.

'We form a long-term business arrangement. Such services, discretely administered, will always be of value to us. A man good at his trade is always useful. It isn't as easy, as you might like to think, to find someone prepared to provide such a service.'

'Who is this fellow you want me to kill?'

'Paolo Sarpi.'

'How do I find him?'

'We don't know where he lives, but he is very well known in Venice, just ask around.'

'To be sure of success, I should take some help. I know that my brother-in-law will help, and he has some friends who could assist with the logistics. Make it four thousand now, and another four after the job.'

'Eight thousand crowns!'

'Do you want the job done or not?'

'Very well, give him the money, Pietro.'

Anthony tiptoed back to the door, locked it behind him, and went back to Hugh's room, using a different route.

'Hugh, Pope Paul is paying Rotilio Orlandini to assassinate Paolo Sarpi,' Anthony whispered, 'I heard him myself.'

'My god. It beggars belief, so it does. Sarpi seemed such a good, gentle person, but what can we do? We can hardly go after him if we're expected to be here to receive our reward the day after tomorrow. I feel responsible in a way. Perhaps if we hadn't discussed that book of Bruno's on Paolo's bookshelf, this wouldn't be happening. I really need that reward, though, so I do. Can we race to warn Sarpi, after we've collected our reward?'

'With a two-day head start, we wouldn't have a hope of catching him. Don't blame yourself, I talked about the book too, and Aldobrandini wrangled Gino's stay with Paolo out of me. I feel so bad about that. It is a dilemma alright.'

'We get our reward or save the life of an innocent man. Perhaps we could save Paolo, and when we get back say that we couldn't collect our reward because we were ill, and went into hiding in case it was the plague, but we're well again now, so could we have our money please. That might do it, so it might.'

'Hugh, they're immoral, not stupid. When news got back that Orlandini had failed, they'd put two and two together and want our heads. We'd have to flee the country. I don't relish explaining to Francesca that our soon to be, God willing, family of seven, assuming she still includes me, will have to flee her native land for heaven knows where, losing everything we have, bar what we can carry.'

'You're right, so you are. There isn't the scrap of an idea on me now. Poor Paolo!'

'Well, I'm going home. Do you want to come, or hang around here?'

'I'll come with you, if I may, so I will?'

PART TWO

CHAPTER NINE

Hugh and Anthony were riding through Frascati.

'I hope that Francesca has forgiven me. I've missed her so much.'

'I'm sure she has, so I am. That's a magnificent palace, so it is.'

'Where?'

'Over there, through the gap in the trees, set in beautiful parkland, so it is,' Hugh said, pointing.

'I'll lay odds that's Aldobrandini's palace. Cardinal Bellarmine told us about it. Don't you remember?'

'Oh yes, now I do. The subsequent events rather made it slip my mind.'

'Damn! I forgot something too.'

'What's that now?'

'I was going to let Rafael Vitale into the pope's library.'

'Whatever for?'

'To look for the missing gospels.'

'What missing gospels is that now?'

'I didn't know, but the disciples did not write the gospels during Christ's lifetime. Most of them were written decades later, by early churchmen who asked those who were around at the time what they remembered. Apparently, the church leaders then spent centuries deciding which ones they wanted, and which they didn't want included in the New Testament. I am intrigued to know what was in the others.'

'Why would that be now?' Hugh asked, puzzled.

'I don't know, Hugh. I suppose it's just that I've never really had my faith tested until recently. Perhaps it's that I've never thought about it. It is comforting to think that your lost loved ones are in heaven, and that you'll join them there one day. But Paolo and Cardinal Bellarmine have made me think. I mean, what do we know about Christ's teaching, with any real certainty?'

'I should let sleeping dogs lie, if I were you.'

'Yes, it's too late now, anyway.'

It was late in the afternoon when Anthony and Hugh rode up the lane leading to Anthony's vineyard. They could see Antonio and Maria practising their wrestling on the grass.

'Anthony, there's your answer. Antonio's a young, fit, intelligent lad, and an excellent fighter, so he is. I'm sure he could beat Orlandini to Venice, if he set off now on your fastest horse.'

'No, don't even think about it, he's my son.'

'Don't think about what, Father?' Antonio and Maria shouted in unison as they stopped fighting and ran over to hug Anthony as he dismounted.

'Oh, I've missed you so much. Is everyone well?'

'Yes, Father, we're all well. Mother's getting plumper by the day. We got the harvest in and the grapes are all pressed and fermenting,' Antonio said. 'Signor Fratelli was quite helpful. We've learnt a few new tricks from him.'

'Is he still here?'

'No, he left as soon as the fermentation was underway.'

'He gave me the creeps,' Maria added. 'The way he looked at me, it was as if he was undressing me with his eyes.'

'You soon put paid to that, Maria. Do you know what she did, Father? She suggested to me that we put on a wrestling display after work one day, on the lawn, while he was watching from the veranda and drinking last year's wine. I thought she was going to tear my arm from its socket. She threw me around like a rag doll.'

'I'd seen him looking at mother the same way, so I told him that it was mother who had taught us wrestling when we were children. I said that her father had been a master of ancient Greek wrestling, and champion of all Tuscany, and that he had taught her. I hope you're not annoyed, Father. I realise it might have been useful for you to speak with him about wine.'

'Of course I'm not annoyed. I'm very grateful. That was ingenious of you, Maria, not to say rather cunning.'

'But what is not to be thought about, Father?' Antonio enquired.

'Forget it! It's not going to happen,' Anthony replied.

'There is a man we met in Venice—'

'Hugh, shut up! He's not going.'

'Father, if it's me you're arguing about, I think I have a right to know.'

'Very well. The man in Venice is Paolo Sarpi, a man we both liked very much. He is a good, kind, intelligent man who the pope and Cardinal Aldobrandini have sent an assassin to kill. We can't go to warn him because we need to be in Rome the day after tomorrow to collect our reward. If Paolo is saved and we aren't around to collect our rewards, it will look very suspicious. Aldobrandini will put two and two together.'

'If a friend of my father's life depends on it, of course I'll go. I've never been to Venice, it'll be a grand adventure.'

'Not a chance, Son, it's far too dangerous. It's out of the question.'

'I agree. It's too dangerous for Antonio. I'll go instead,' Maria chipped in.

'I'm not letting my twin sister go instead of me.'

'Well, why not? I beat you at wrestling half the time, and I'd appear less threatening. This assassin wouldn't expect me to be his nemesis.'

'No, absolutely not. Neither of you are going,' Anthony said.

'They have a point, Anthony, so they do. You said yourself that Maria can throw a man twice her weight. A teenage brother and sister would attract little attention, and they can watch each other's back, so they can. You know it's the only way to save the life of a good man, but we can't keep arguing about it. It's now that they need to start, if they're to have any chance.'

'No, Francesca would kill me! I absolutely forbid it. Now can we please go inside? I'm desperate to see Francesca.'

Through the kitchen window, Francesca saw Anthony approaching the door and rushed out to meet him. She threw her arms around him, and they kissed, long and passionately. She ran her fingers through his hair.

'You're hurt.'

'It's nothing much, it will soon heal.'

'Thank God you're home. There isn't a minute I haven't thought about you, worried about what dangers you might face.'

'Well, I'm here now, and it's all over. You won't mind if Hugh stays a day or two, do you? He saved my life.'

'Oh heavens, I knew it. I knew you'd be in danger.'

'It was a stupid lapse of attention, entirely my fault, and Hugh really did save my life, well he and the Swiss Guard.'

'In that case, yes, of course. Is that Cardinal Aldibrandy with you too?'

'Aldobrandini, no he's in Rome.'

'Good, I didn't like him.'

'You're a fine judge of character, darling.'

'We'll have a chicken for dinner. There's one that hasn't been laying lately. I'll wring its neck. I'll pretend it's that cardinal.'

Francesca made a chicken and pasta dish in a white

wine sauce. After dinner, she took the younger children to bed whilst Anthony fetched another flagon of wine. He filled everyone's goblets before sitting down again.

'You must tell us all about your adventures, Father,' Maria said.

'It's rather a long story, and there are parts of it I'd rather forget.'

'Oh, away with you man, it's a great story, so it is. Your father had the genius on him. He worked it out that the murders were connected to the sun standing still, and the earth circling around it. So off we were to Padua, to talk to a professor there, who believes that to be true. Worked through a list of his former students we did and established where they were to on the nights of the murders. An Englishman it turned out to be and shot he was before he managed to—'

'That's enough, Hugh! They don't need to know the details.'

'Then at least you can tell us about this Paolo fellow. Why do you both like him, and why does the pope want him killed?' Antonio asked.

'It's easier to answer the second question than the first,' Antony said, taking a long draught of wine. 'The Venetians have challenged the authority of the pope over civil matters, like making corrupt priests submit to civil courts.'

'Corrupt priests, Father?'

'Oh my lord, you wouldn't believe some of the things we've learnt about corruption in the church, and I'm not going to tell you, not the most sordid bits, anyway. You know that enormous palace, set back on the road just outside Frascati?'

'Yes, Father,' Maria and Antonio replied in unison.

'That belongs to Cardinal Aldobrandini. It's his country villa, which he hardly ever uses, apparently, and he has an even bigger palace in Rome. They're all in it for the money. It's a huge revenue generating machine. Anyway, where was I? Oh yes, the Venetians have appointed Paolo Sarpi to negotiate with the church and represent them legally. He has the most incredible intelligence, what a mind. The cardinal kept trying to implicate him in the murders which we were investigating, but it was amply clear that he had nothing to do with them. He may be arguing Venice's case against the pope, but he does it lawfully. He is clearly a man of peace, and tolerant of other faiths. But the pope has sent an assassin to kill him.'

'Who, Father?' Maria asked.

'One of the men who was killing the priests.' Anthony drained his goblet and refilled it. 'If we hadn't found the killers, well, I don't know. It's all such a mess. I probably gave him the idea.'

'Gave who the idea, Father?' Maria asked again, softly.

'Aldobrandini, the pope, both of them. I was so shocked at him murdering for money, but they... they thought they could use him. I was wandering around the pope's palace, unable to sleep, and discovered that they'd had him brought up from the dungeons and were negotiating the price for killing Paolo.'

'They'd have had the idea in them without yourself now. You shouldn't be blaming yourself.'

'Oh Hugh, but I couldn't keep my mouth shut about that book Paolo had, or about his having Gino to stay with him when he went to Venice. Bit by bit I fed their frenzied fanaticism.'

'Darling, I think you should go to bed,' Francesca suggested as she returned to the table. 'You've obviously had a tiring journey. Come up with me, you can keep me warm, I've missed you so much.'

'Perhaps you're right, Francesca. I am feeling rather weary.'

'Yes, I'll help you up the stairs. Hugh, the room you had last time is free for you. I've lit the fire. Maria, Antonio, just take the plates back to the kitchen and I'll deal with them in the morning. Don't forget to blow the lamps out before you go to bed.' With that, she helped Anthony stand up and led him upstairs. Hugh gave them a few minutes before he went to bed, too. Antonio started clearing the plates, while Maria sat pensively, twirling her hair through her fingers.

'Are you going to let me clear up alone?'

'No, sorry, Antonio.' She got up and helped him clear up. 'I'm not tired yet, I'll clean the dishes.'

'I'll help.'

'He's changed hasn't he, Father that is?'

'Yes.'

'I'm worried about him. If they kill this Paolo, he'll blame himself.'

'He already does.'

'I think we should save him. Set off at the first cock-crow. What do you say, Antonio?'

'I say yes. Father can look after the wine now.' They

finished the remaining washing up in silence.

'Antonio, I'm going to write them a note for the morning. You see if Hugh's asleep yet. If necessary, wake him up. We need to know where to find Paolo.'

'All right, Maria.'

Antonio turned the handle of the guest bedroom and tiptoed in. He crossed to the bed. Hugh was snoring softly. He put his hand on Hugh's shoulder and gently rocked him.

'Hugh, it's Antonio, wake up!'

'What the blazes.'

'Shh! We've decided to go, like you said, to save Paolo. We need to know where to find him.'

'Ah, may the good lord with you be, now. That's grand, so it is. The man to be warned is Paolo Sarpi. He's about the same age as your father, an inch or so shorter, slim and with a remarkably high forehead. It's piercing brown eyes he has on him, and will be wearing the black robes of the Servite order. It's in a house on the canal front he lives, three doors past the Ducal Palace from where you get off the ferry, near Saint Mark's square in Venice. Head to Rome, then Florence, Bologna, Padua and Venice. Keep your eyes open for a fellow named Rotilio Orlandini. He's the assassin, so he is, although he probably won't be using that name. He's about my height and build. I remember his eyes looked odd, so they did, sort of recessed in their sockets a bit, as if he didn't get enough sleep. He will have a few others with himself. Pass me my purse, would you, lad.' Antonio looked around and passed him the purse on the window ledge.

Hugh felt inside the purse and took out some gold coins. 'Here's thirty ducats each, which is more than enough for board and lodging there and back, so it is. Good luck, and come back safe. Oh, one more thing there is. On the way back, look in on a man named Gino Torelli, so you should. He has a farm two miles south of Monselice, on the Ferrara road. The pope has sent inquisitors to him. He thinks Gino may have been working with Paolo, but it's innocent that he is. It will be a great comfort to your father, and myself, if he is alive. Lord bless you, a good lad you are, to be sure.'

While Antonio was with Hugh, Maria wrote a note for their parents. She made it as clear as she could that it was their decision to go, and nobody else's.

CHAPTER TEN

'Isn't it exciting to get away from the villa, and see a bit of the world?' Maria yelled as they galloped northwards from Rome.

'It will be,'

'What do you mean, Antonio?'

'Our world has been Florence, Frascati, a couple of days in Rome, and the roads in between. We're still on a road we've already travelled,' Antonio yelled back. 'Once we get past Florence, we'll be beyond the edge of our world, as we've known it. I'm really looking forward to Venice.'

'Me too, with a tinge of trepidation. Do you think we could slow down a bit now? Allegro's tiring.' Maria called out and Antonio reined Bellezza in, then they settled into a steady trot.

'What do you want to do with your life, Maria?'

'Mother wants me to marry a count, or a rich banker; I'd rather go to sea. Father has seen so much of the world, and he talks so nostalgically about his time at sea. I think I might like to marry a sea captain, one who can take me around the world with him.'

'I don't think they take girls on ships. Father said it was bad luck.'

'Then I'll cut my hair, and bind my breasts tightly, and join a pirate ship,' Maria said in her deepest voice. 'What are you going to do?'

'Well, I suppose there's the vineyard. It's certainly a lot more pleasant than working in the forge. That seems such a very distant memory now.'

'How far do you think we can stretch thirty ducats? What's that in crowns?' Maria asked.

'I don't know for sure. I think there are hundreds of crowns to a ducat.'

'Wow, we have a fortune. Do you know how much we'll need to stay at an inn?'

'Of course not, neither of us have been away from home before.'

'Well, let's try to stretch our money out as much as we can. I'd like to save up my own fortune, so that I can really see the world. Maybe I could buy my own ship, if sea captains won't take girls to sea.'

'Okay, we could maybe find a barn to sleep in some nights.'

'Good idea, and take a single room with twin beds every other night. I don't think I want to rough it every night.'

Anthony arrived once more at the Quirinal Palace, a little before noon on Wednesday, the twenty-third of

September. Sergeant Hennard met him at the main gate.

'It's very good to see you again, sir. I'll take you to the foyer of the great hall. Earl Hugh is already there.' As they walked towards the great hall, Anthony noticed that everything seemed to have been tidied. There wasn't a speck of dust anywhere. Every painting was perfectly level, every servant was in their best tunic, every ornament was in place. Hugh stood up from his chair as Anthony and Hennard entered the foyer. 'Someone will call you into the hall when they've finished the business of the consistory. I'll have to get back to the main gate. I hope I'll see you both again before you leave.' Sergeant Hennard closed the door and left them alone.

'Anthony, you're looking much better, so you are.'

'Thank you, Hugh, I'm felling better too. But I'm so desperately worried about Maria and Antonio. Maria left a note saying that she and Antonio made their own decision to go. But I do wish you hadn't put the thought in their impetuous, young heads. Francesca certainly blames you. I suppose you're the nearest stranger, the scapegoat.'

'I'm sorry. I thought it was for the best, so I did. You know you'd never be able to live with yourself if Paolo were murdered. I'm sure they'll be fine. They've had the best teacher. I mean that, I do really.' Anthony sat down and Hugh sat down beside him. They sat in silence for a few minutes.

'I'm just so worried about them, Hugh.'

'I'm sure they will beat Orlandini to Venice. They're much younger than him, so they are,' Hugh whispered.

'But if he was released straight after I overheard that

171

conversation, then it took us what, three hours to ride back to the villa? He'll have at least a six-hour head start on them.'

'But he's got to enlist his brother-in-law and his friends, so he has. That will take time. They'll probably argue about how they'll split the money, amongst other things. Rome to Venice is about an eight, maybe seven-day ride. That's enough time to make up a few hours, so it is.' Before Anthony could reply, the doors of the great hall opened, and Cardinal Aldobrandini emerged.

'Earl O'Neill, Sir Anthony, welcome. We are ready for you now. Please follow me.' They entered a lavishly decorated hall with a painted ceiling. There were paintings of biblical scenes hanging on one of the long walls, and portraits down the other. Anthony recognised the nearest portrait as Pope Paul, and the next but one as Pope Clement, so he assumed they must all be popes. Pope Paul sat on a throne, set upon a platform, at the far end of the hall. There was a chest beside the throne. Cardinal Aldobrandini led them down an aisle, between rows of chairs, towards the platform. Anthony counted the rows and estimated there must be fifty to sixty cardinals in attendance. When they reached the front, Aldobrandini indicated three vacant chairs in the front row. They sat and Aldobrandini took the third. Pope Paul rose from his throne and began his address.

'Two men, to whom we all owe a great debt, have joined us. I shall not name them. We shall know them simply as the Englishman and the Irishman. Some of you may have heard rumours, which with great sadness I must now confirm. There has been a devil incarnate who has been murdering priests, in their churches, on saint's days. We must pray for the souls of Father Caprona, from Ferrara, Father Valenti, from Monselice and Abbot Fontana of Bologna. We are lucky to have with us Cardinal Pinelli, who had the most narrow of escapes. We pray also for the soul of his tailor. This devil was working his way towards Rome, we believe, with the intention of more murders. Thankfully, Cardinal Aldobrandini heard the confession of Pope Clement, on his deathbed, who told him of the Englishman, a most talented man. A man who we should call upon in our hour of direst need. By God's divine will, there was also in Rome the Irishman, a man of complementary talents who was already acquainted with the Englishman. Together, and with the help of the Swiss Guard, they tracked down the devil, and slew him. For so long as God may decree, they have, by God's grace, brought peace once more. I do not name them, for we may need their services again, though I pray not. And if we do, then a degree of anonymity is useful to their work. Gentlemen, please accept our thanks, our prayers, and a small token of our gratitude.' Aldobrandini stood up and beckoned to Anthony and Hugh to stand too. Aldobrandini led them up onto the stage. Pope Paul held out his hand for each of them to kiss. Aldobrandini opened the chest and took out two sacks, which he passed, one by one, to the pope. The pope presented the first one to Anthony, and the second one to Hugh.

'It's all there. You can count it afterwards,' whispered Aldobrandini.

'Let us signal our appreciation of our gallant knights,' Pope Paul said, signalling the cardinals to stand and starting the applause. It felt like an hour, but was probably only a minute, before the applause died down and Aldobrandini led them back to the foyer.

'I must return to business, but once again, Sir Anthony and Earl O'Neill, thank you.' He slid back through the doors and Anthony and Hugh were alone again, weighing their sacks in their hands.

'Would it be poor form to open them and check, now would it?' Hugh asked.

'There's nobody about,' Anthony said, sitting down and opening his sack. He began counting out the gold ten-ducat pieces into piles of ten. Hugh did the same. 'I've got two hundred ten-ducat pieces. How about you?'

'The same. What are you going to do now?'

'Every fibre of my being urges me to ride to Venice. But at the same time, Francesca is pregnant and alone with little William and baby Anna. It's best I get home. I'm sorry, but she left me with instructions that you're not welcome.'

'I understand. After everything we've been through, shall we just find an inn and have one last drink first?'

'I'd like that, but do you think it's wise to carry this much money?'

'I think we can trust Sergeant Hennard, so we can. Let's leave it with him and collect it afterwards.'

They went to an inn they had passed on the night of their patrol, took a table in a quiet corner, and ordered wine.

'So Pope Paul thinks he may use your services again, Anthony. How do you like being on the same payroll as

Orlandini?'

'Not one bit, Hugh. We set out to track down a satanic killer of innocent priests. Well, I have to say that even when Brown had the lit taper in his hand, about to burn me to death, I felt a tiny sliver of sympathy for him. That speech the pope made was pure hypocrisy, from beginning to end. Praying for the souls of the murdered priests, for example. How can he believe in an immortal soul and hire an assassin to kill an innocent man? How can he not believe he will burn in hell himself? He simply can't believe in an immortal soul.'

'Or he believes that he's justified it, in some way.'

'How?'

'Perhaps he thinks Paolo is a threat to God's church.'

'I don't see how. He's simply a threat to the civil power of the church in Venice, not its religious power. Paolo took holy orders himself. He may not believe in an immortal soul in the same way, but he doesn't prevent anyone else from believing. The same could be said of Cardinal Bellarmine.'

'I think power deforms a man, so it does. Everyone defers to you. Nobody questions you. What you want starts to become what you need. The more powerful you become, the more your enemies envy you. Then if you show any sign of weakness, they pounce on you, so they do.'

'What do you believe, Hugh? Do you believe in your immortal soul?'

'I do.'

'How many men have you killed?'

'Too many to count, so it is. But they'd all have killed

me, if I hadn't killed them first. What about you?'

'I'd like to think I could count them, but when I was with the Sea Beggars, and firing canister shot into the Spanish troops approaching us across the ice, no, there is no way I could count them. But as you say, I was fighting for my own life, and those of my shipmates.'

'So do you believe in your immortal soul?'

'I don't know now. It has been a comfort, and I feel such a cleansing of the spirit after confession. But after talking to Paolo and Cardinal Bellarmine, I don't think I do anymore, at least not in the same way as I did.'

'How do you mean?'

'Well, I imagined we would live an afterlife, not playing the harp sitting on a cloud, but carrying on in my ghostly body, talking to my dead parents about things, looking down on, and perhaps looking after my children. But if Christ himself needed his mortal body to be resurrected, in order to be recognisable to the disciples: if the son of God could not wield his immortal soul to present himself, then what I've thought about souls or ghosts is holed below the waterline.'

'But do you still believe in God?'

'Absolutely.'

'So what is God?'

'Well, we exist, the Earth and the sun, whichever orbits the other, exist, and it all had to start somewhere, right?'

'Yes. So God created the heavens and the earth and all the plants and creatures.'

'And who created God?'

'God always existed. You just have to believe. That's

what they say, so they do.'

'And I struggle with that, Hugh. But I see it like this. Let's say that before time there was nothing, but that nothing was, kind of unstable. It was made up of some kind of credit and some kind of equal and opposite debit. Credit cannot exist without debit. There is a bond between them. Equally, since they cancel each other out, they need to be apart to exist. Therefore nothing, the balance that is, exploded. We may live in the credit universe or the debit universe. But however you look at it, the universe is so immense, so complex, so wonderful, that if this credit or debit universe is God, then God is truly wondrous, and a pleasure to be part of. Have you ever looked in the eye of a creature, a dog, cat or horse perhaps, and recognised that we're all intrinsically part of the same thing? Have you sat a while, watching a plant orientate its leaves toward the sun?'

'I can't say that I have. Where does that leave us with killing innocents? No immortal soul, no need to worry about burning in hell.'

'It means we're all part of the same wonderful creation. One thing I learnt, serving at sea, is that we're all in the same boat, and we need to work together, to help each other, because we are all better off that way.'

'Have you finished now?'

'Yes.'

'Then let's drink up, get our loot, and get going. Tell Francesca I'm sorry. I hope we'll meet again someday, hopefully not doing Pope Paul's dirty work.'

Antonio and Maria rode northwards from Rome. The

suburbs dwindled into small villages and hamlets, then forested hillsides and open farmland. Whenever they passed an unwalled field, or a stream with grassy banks, they were forced to yield to the needs of Allegro and Bellezza, and let them drink and graze. At these grazing stops, Antonio and Maria would take the leather water pouches from their saddlebags, drink, and refill them if there was a stream. They would take the bread and cheese out too, and refresh themselves. Maria found some wild garlic and added it to enhance the flavour of her cheese.

'Well, this is all very restful, but I wonder how far in front of us these assassins are?' Maria mused, twirling a stalk of grass between her teeth.

'The horses have to eat.'

'I know. Do you think they've had enough yet?' Maria stood up and paced over to Allegro. She tried to mount him, but he turned to prevent her. 'It appears not,' she said, lying down again on the grass beside Antonio. 'At this rate, I doubt we'll make it to Fiano Romano by nightfall. Perhaps we'll try finding a barn or something to sleep in tonight.'

'We can try.'

The sun was gliding towards the horizon, and there was no sign of Fiano Romano yet.

'That looks like a farmhouse over there,' Maria said, pointing. After another half mile or so, they could see outbuildings. 'There's one lamp burning in the farmhouse, but that's on the side facing away from the outbuildings.'

'Yes, and the moon has already risen. If we skirt

around the edge of that field, we could approach the barn without being seen from the farmhouse. What do you think?'

'Well, I don't fancy sleeping by the side of the road.' They rode around the edge of the field and approached the barn. They dismounted. 'The door is only secured with a wooden wedge. I'll open it and you lead the horses in,' Maria whispered. Once they were inside, Maria pulled the door almost shut, knelt down and reached through the gap to push the wedge in, leaving the door just a few inches ajar. As their eyes adjusted to the moonlight seeping through the gaps in the timber walls and roof, they made out stacks of straw bales and some sacks, a rusty plough, equally rusty forks, scythes and other assorted farm implements. 'I don't think this farm is in its prime, do you?' Maria whispered.

'No, but it'll suit us well enough,' Antonio replied, taking the saddle and saddle bag from Bellezza, gently taking the bit from her mouth as he removed her bridle. Maria did the same with Allegro. When he was done, Antonio flopped onto a pile of straw. 'I must say, this is quite comfortable, and warm.' Maria flopped down beside him.

'A little itchy, though. We must get away before first light. We don't want the farmer finding us.'

'No', Antonio replied sleepily. The sooner we get to sleep, the sooner we'll be away.'

'Good night, Antonio.'

'Good night, Maria.' Several hours later, the moon set and the barn was in total darkness. Only the occasional hoot of an owl broke the silence: the twins slept soundly.

With the first of morning twilight, Maria was awoken by a strange noise.

'What's that?' she whispered. Antonio didn't stir. His breathing was soft and steady. Maria gently climbed down from the hay and felt her way towards the sound. She could make out the outline of a horse and the noise was getting closer. 'Is that you, Allegro?' She made her way towards the horse's head. 'It is you Allegro, what are you doing?' She ran her hands gently down his mane. 'What's this, a sack?' Allegro nuzzled into the sack again and began chomping. Maria put her hand into the sack. 'Carrots, you do like your carrots, don't you? Well, we'd better get going, it'll be dawn soon.' She made her way back to Antonio and shook him.

'What's up?'

'It'll soon be dawn. We need to get going.'

'All right. What's that noise?'

'Allegro has found a bag of carrots and ripped it open with his teeth. You know how he likes carrots. Hey, if we take carrots with us, we can reach behind us into our saddlebags, pull out a carrot, and feed the horses on the go. We won't have to keep stopping every hour or so.'

'Then there won't be as much room for bread and cheese.'

'You saddle and bridle the horses and I'll think about it. There's a bit of rope over here. Have you got your knife?' Antonio passed her his knife, then saddled Bellezza. 'Here are some smaller empty sacks.' She took some sacks and made holes near the open end. Then she threaded the rope through and put knots in the ends. She took two more sacks and did the same. Then she started stuffing carrots from the large sack into the small sacks, by which time Antonio had saddled and harnessed both horses. 'Right, how about this.' Maria took two of the smaller bags, joined by a length of rope and slung them across Allegro's neck so that the rope rested against the pommel of the saddle, with a carrot holster on either side. She passed the other set of joined sacks to Antonio.

'That's not a bad idea, Maria. Now let's go.'

'Not yet. Can you get a ducat out of your purse? We ought to leave the farmer something for the carrots.'

'What's wrong with your purse?'

'It was my idea, and I'm saving up for a boat, don't forget.'

CHAPTER ELEVEN

They arrived in Orvieto after a long ride, just after sunset.

'I know I said I wanted to save our money, Antonio, but I don't think I can face sleeping rough again tonight. This looks like a pleasant town. Let's find an inn here. Then we'll get an idea of what things cost and be able to budget accordingly.'

'Good idea. What do you think of the look of that inn over there?'

'Let's try it. Wait a moment though, I've had a thought, Antonio. Whether we are successful or not, we mustn't let slip who we are. After all, Father couldn't do what we're doing, because we would have had to flee the country. If the pope learns of our role, should we be successful, then surely the outcome will be much the same.'

'You're right. What shall we call each other?' Antonio asked.

'Let's keep it simple, call each other brother and sister.'

'That's all very well in conversation, but we're about to check into an inn. Do you think they'll want to know our names?'

'Good point, Brother. Father often talks about Anthony and Francis Bacon, so how about if you become Francis Pancetta, and I'm your sister, Antonia Pancetta?' Antonio laughed and they dismounted outside the inn, and tied their horses' reins to a rail. Then they went inside. There were several tables with people eating, and the food smelt good. There was a log fire burning, and a counter from which a man was dispensing drinks. Antonio assumed he was the innkeeper. Antonio approached him, followed by Maria. The innkeeper put down the crate he was carrying and squinted at them.

'Could we have a room with twin beds for the night, please? I'm travelling with my sister.'

'I've heard that one before. We run a respectable house here. Have you got a wedding certificate? Show me your wedding rings.'

'I am his sister, sir. We're twins, in fact. Can't you see?'

'Where did I put my glasses? I had them earlier.' The innkeeper felt around on the shelf behind the bar. 'Ah, here they are,' he said, perching the glasses on the bridge of his nose. 'My word, yes. I see what you mean. Well, in that case, yes, we have a twin room. Two crowns in advance. That includes stabling, water and fodder for your horses, dinner, as much wine as you can drink, and breakfast. Do you have two crowns?'

'I have a ducat.'

'Haven't you got anything smaller?'

'No, sir, I'm afraid we don't.'

'All right, give it here and I'll send the boy to the bank

while I show you the room. Have you got any bags?'

'No sir, we're travelling light.'

'A ducat indeed, and no luggage. I've never heard the like. Michael, come here. Take this gentleman's ducat. Wake up Tornelli, the bank manager, and get a sackful of change. Be quick about it. Follow me, sir, madam, the room is this way. I'll get Michael to look after your horses when he gets back.' The innkeeper picked up an oil lamp and some tapers and led them upstairs, and along a corridor. He opened a door, led them in, and put the oil lamp down on a chest of drawers. There was a large bed frame with a straw mattress at one end of the room, next to a fireplace. There were kindling and logs already in the grate, and a basket of logs next to the fire. The innkeeper went across to the bed, reached underneath it and pulled out a smaller truckle bed. 'I imagine you will use the truckle bed, signor.' He lit a taper from the oil lamp and soon had the fire blazing. 'I'll leave you the oil lamp. If you need the facilities, there's a privy in the garden. If the queue is too long, or you don't want to go outside, there's a chamber pot in the cupboard under the window. Have a good evening. Dinner service will start in half an hour,' the innkeeper said as he closed the door behind him.

'I trust that farmer is happier with the ducat we left him, for a few carrots,' Antonio whispered to Maria.

'Yes all right, we're learning.'

They arrived in Florence on Saturday, the twenty-sixth of September. They rode in silence for a while, each knowing what their twin was thinking, as they took in the sights, sounds and smells of their childhood.

'We shouldn't.' Maria said. 'I'd love to look around our old house again, but the neighbours would recognise us, and however long it took to reach the pope, he might eventually guess what our mission had been.'

'I know, and I'd like to see the forge where I worked, and see my old friends. It makes you think, though, how hard life was before father arrived. We weren't at all grateful were we, well I wasn't, anyway.'

'He was a stranger. We were fifteen. We'd heard about him from mother, but we resented the fact that he hadn't been there for us. Knowing that he had to leave to save his skin, and knowing now why he hadn't returned for so long, doesn't change that sense of abandonment.'

'No, but I'm glad we have the vineyard, and that I don't have to work in the forge anymore.'

'He's changed everything. We have a future now. We've learnt so much and we will soon see a whole new world. Shall we stay in the inn near the Basilica of Saint Mary of the Flower?'

'I thought you wanted to save your fortune: that's the best inn in the city.'

'Which is why we're unlikely to meet any of our childhood acquaintances there. I feel like a little luxury and fine food for a change.'

As they rode out of Florence and headed north, the road up the valley narrowed, and the mountains closed in on either side. The city had long since receded behind them, and their pace slowed as the climb steepened. There were no other travellers to be seen, but the birdsong, from the tree-lined slopes on either side, seemed amplified by the mountains.

'What a beautiful day,' Maria called out, her words echoing around the valley.

'Isn't it? I often used to wonder what these mountains were like, when we were young. I had no idea they were as beautiful as this. Do you know how far they stretch?'

'The innkeeper said as far as Bologna, which is just over sixty miles. We'll do well to make it there in three days over the mountains.'

'Did he mention any places to stay on the way?'

'We should reach Barberino by nightfall. Then there's Castiglione and Vado before we get to Bologna.'

'Do you hear that?'

'Hear what?'

'Exactly! The birds have stopped singing, and Belleza keeps twitching, for some reason.'

'Allegro doesn't seem himself either. My vision is getting blurred.'

'Mine too. My God, look out!' Antonio shouted as Belleza reared up and threw him to the ground. Allegro reared too, throwing Maria from the saddle. The horses turned and bolted back the way they had come. Antonio crawled over to Maria, as boulders came crashing down the slopes on either side of them, smashing the trees to splinters. 'What's happening?'

'It's an earthquake. What should we do?'

'Over there, between those two enormous boulders, there's a gap. If we get in the gap, the boulders may shield us from other boulders. Let's go!' They sprinted over to the gap and crawled in. The fury of the rockfall was deafening, and the dust was choking them. They pressed further into the gap as boulders cascaded into them. The world grew darker and darker until the shaking stopped as quickly as it had started. 'Are you all right, Maria?' Antonio gasped, between coughing fits.

'I think so. Can you move? You're on top of me.'

'I'll try, but I think we're trapped. I can only see a small sliver of daylight. Antonio wriggled towards the light.'

'Ouch, that hurt.'

'I'm sorry,' Antonio said, as he pushed at rocks and boulders that surrounded the small aperture letting light in. 'Can you move a bit? I want to brace my back against the rock behind you so that I can push with my legs against whatever's covering the gap.' Maria wriggled around him.

'Let's both push.' Their legs trembled with the effort. 'I think something's giving.'

'I think my legs are.'

'Shut up and push. Yes, it's going. One more, yes.'

'Can we try to move that one now?' They braced themselves for an attempt at moving another rock. They heaved with all their might. 'No, it's no good. It's a small gap. Do you think we could crawl through it?'

'Let me try, my shoulders are smaller than yours.' Antonio wriggled around Maria to let her have a try at climbing out. 'Jesus! No, I can't get through.'

'Try twisting onto your back. The gap seems to curve upwards a bit. I think on your back you might be able to work with the curve, rather than against it.'

'I'll try,' Maria writhed around, 'can you push me a bit? Yes, I think I'm moving. Yes, oh thank god, I'm out,'

Maria poked her head back through the gap. 'Are you coming?'

'If I poke my arms out, can you pull?' Maria pulled as hard as she could, but Antonio was too big for the gap. 'It's no good. It's too small. You might have to go and fetch help.'

'I don't like to worry you, but there's no sign of the horses, and the road is blocked on either side of us. Wait there, I've had an idea.'

'Wait here? Where the hell do you think I'm going to go? What are you doing?'

'I'm going to look for a suitable tree branch. I think I might be able to move this rock, if I can apply some leverage to it.' A few minutes later, she returned with a branch. 'Have you got your knife on you?'

'Yes.'

'Can you pass it to me? The end of this branch is a little too thick to go in the crack I want to lever at.' Antonio passed his knife through the gap. After a few more minutes, Antonio heard Maria straining at the lever. He could see the rock she was trying to move, so he wriggled into a position where he could push at it with his legs too. He waited until he heard the strain of Maria's effort and pushed with everything he had. He felt the rock move, but only half an inch or so. 'I felt it move a bit, did you?'

'I think so.'

'Okay, let's have another go. On the count of three. One, two, heave!' Antonio pushed as Maria pulled. Antonio heard the sickening snap of the branch breaking.

'Shit! It's broken.'

'Well, it moved a bit. Let me have another go at squeezing through. You pull my arms.' He felt as though his arms were being pulled from their sockets. He writhed and struggled to breathe as the rock pressed against his chest; and prevented him from taking a full breath for the next push. He pushed as hard as he could, then he sensed darkness falling. As he opened his eyes, Maria was kneeling over him. She got up and put her hand out to help pull him up.

'You must have passed out. You stopped breathing. I guess without air, your chest became just that little smaller, and I pulled you free. I slapped you around a bit, and you woke up.' Antonio shook dust from his hair and looked around. The road had become a sea of boulders and felled trees.

'I know they buried us alive, but if we hadn't been between those boulders, they would have flattened us.'

'You're right, it was a good call, Brother. Even so, I thought I'd lost you just now.'

'So what do we do now?' Antonio asked.

'The horses bolted and galloped back down the road. They seemed to sense the earthquake, before we did.'

'That's right, and the birds went quiet.'

'We seem to have two choices. Clamber over these boulders down the mountain pass, away from our destination; or clamber up the pass, the way we were heading. We don't know how far we have to climb before the road is clear. It may take us two or three days, possibly more, to get to Barberino. When we get there, we don't know if we'll be able to buy fresh horses, or whether we can afford them. Florence is much closer, and we may find Allegro and Belleza on the way, if they survived. If they got clear of the earthquake, they'd stop at the nearest good grazing.'

'Down it is then,' Antonio agreed, and they scrambled over and between the boulders and the trees. The sun was setting, and they had not yet cleared the boulder-field. 'Maria, if we carry on much further in the dark, one of us is going to break an ankle, or worse.'

'I agree. I've seen a few clefts in the mountainside. If we find a suitable cave, we could sleep rough, maybe make a fire.'

'A cave sounds good, and there's no shortage of wood around, but what would we light it with? Did you bring a steel and flint?'

'No. Can you rub two sticks together?'

'I tried that when I was a boy. You need something like a bow, to turn one stick really fast. It would be dawn before we had a fire going.'

'So we just huddle together for warmth. How about up there? Does that look like a cave to you?'

'It looks like there are several, large and small. Let's go and take a closer look.' They clambered up the mountainside and found several clefts and caves. 'What about this one? The opening is facing away from the wind. I can't see any animal bones that would suggest it might be a wolf's lair.'

'Oh, thanks for that, Brother, I hadn't thought of wolves. We're going to get a great night's sleep now. When we do get back to Florence, I suggest we invest some of our money in a flint and steel, maybe some gunpowder as well, to get a fire started. If this can happen once, it can happen again. So I know it was my idea to sleep rough some nights, and save our money, but we need to be prepared for it. I'm thirsty. Have you got your water pouch?'

'No, mine was in my saddle bag.'

'Shit, mine too. Well, let's try to get some rest anyway, and hope we find a stream in the morning.'

Antonio awoke, chilled to the bone. He was curled around Maria for warmth, but she felt cold, too. His mouth was dry. He tried to generate some saliva, but nothing would come. Morning twilight crept into the cave.

'Maria, Maria, wake up,' he said, shaking her.

'Urrgh.'

'Maria, I think we should get moving. It'll warm us up, and the sun will rise soon, but we need to find some water.'

'Yes, I'm so cold.'

'I know. Come on, get up.' Antonio stood up and helped Maria to her feet. Their movements were unsteady at first, and they took the scramble down the mountainside. Step by step, they felt warmer, but their thirst became unbearable.

'I can't go on, Brother.'

'You have to.'

'No.' Maria slumped down into a hollow between two rocks. 'I'm going to take a little nap.'

'For God's sake, Maria, wake up!' he screamed, shaking her. But it was useless. Antonio left Maria and continued the descent. The sun crept above the mountain ridge to his left. 'How much further?' he said to himself and slipped going over a boulder. 'Shit! well, nothing broken. Gotta keep going, gotta keep going,' he staggered on, 'think the rocks getting smaller, maybe, gotta keep going.' He stumbled faster and faster and then fell flat on his face. He felt himself slipping off to sleep. Then he felt a gentle vibration of the ground. 'What's that?' he said into the dust, as he felt something rasping at the back of his neck. He rolled onto his back, struggling to focus. Gradually, the tongue of Belleza came into focus. He staggered to his feet, using her reins to pull himself up. He felt his way around her until he got to his saddlebag. His fingers trembling, he undid the buckle, and reached inside for his leather water pouch. He took out the cork and took a sip. Then he drank more until he had drained it. He looked around. Allegro was a short distance away, in a wooded-glade, grazing. He ran over to her and took Maria's water pouch from her saddlebag. 'Stay here! We'll be back soon.' Antonio ran back the way he had come. The boulder-field slowed him again, but he soon found Maria motionless. He uncorked her pouch and dribbled a few drops onto her lips. There was no response. He dribbled a few more and her mouth opened slightly. Her tongue felt around her lips. He dribbled more into her open mouth. She coughed. Her eyes opened, she grabbed the flask from him, sat up, threw her head back and drank. 'I found the horses.'

'So it seems.'

'Can you walk?'

'Yes, I think so. Is it far?'

'No, not too far. They found a glade to graze in.'

'Okay, let's go. I hope there's a stream too.'

They scrambled their way over the boulder-field and settled into a steady walk, as the road became easier. Allegro and Belleza were grazing contentedly where Antonio had left them. Maria went to Allegro and felt into her saddlebag. She pulled out some bread and cheese and began gnawing it. Antonio recovered his bread and cheese from Belleza's saddlebag and did the same. He looked around and could see hoof prints running through the glade. He followed them.

'Where are you going?' Maria called out.

'I'm just going to see where these lead.'

He returned ten minutes later. 'They found a stream. Give me your flask.' He disappeared back into the glade and re-emerged a quarter of an hour later, with refilled flasks. 'Are you ready to ride back to Florence?'

'Yes, I'm much better now.'

'I thought you were dead.'

'So did I.'

They rode into Florence mid-afternoon.

'We might as well stay at the same inn as the night before last,' Maria suggested. 'The food was good, and I'm famished.'

'Me too. Shall we do our shopping first, or after we've checked in?'

'Let's check in first, get the horses stabled, have a snack, and discuss what we need.' Antonio nodded agreement, and they made their way to the inn.

'Hello again. I didn't expect to see you back so soon,'

the innkeeper said as they entered. 'Shall I prepare some baths for you, and you may like some laundry, perhaps?'

'Yes, please. There was an earthquake as we made our way up the mountain pass, towards Barberino. We were lucky to make it back.'

'We felt some minor tremors here, but nothing serious.'

'Well, the pass to Barberino is completely blocked. Is there another way?'

'It's further, but if you take the road to Pistoia, and then the mountain pass via Spedaletto and San Pellegrino, that remains open more often than the Barberino route.'

'How much further is it?' Antonio asked.

'Half a day, perhaps.'

'Well, that's not as bad as I feared. Sister, how can we have our clothes laundered, and do our shopping, if we don't have a change of clothes?'

'Good point, and I'm starving.'

'If I may suggest, tell me what shopping you need, and I will have it done. I will bring some nightshirts to your room, as well as a bathtub and hot water, some bread, butter and salami. Put your dirty clothes outside the door, and I will have them laundered and repaired. They will dry quickly over the stove in the kitchen. I will bring them up to you when they are ready. Now what else do you need?'

'A flint and steel, and a small pouch of gunpowder. We almost froze to death in the mountains.'

'And a couple of blankets. I think we could fit those in the saddlebags, Brother.'

'Yes, and some bread and cheese to take with us

tomorrow, please.'

'Of course. Shall we say a florin to cover everything?'

'Yes, that seems very reasonable. Could you pay the gentleman please, Brother?'

Maria was enjoying her soak in the bathtub. Antonio was sitting on his bed, eating his bread and salami.

'Is it worth going on, Maria? We will have lost two and a half days, at least. I'm not sure we have a chance of catching Orlandini now.'

'How do we know we hadn't already overtaken him? He may be turning back from the rockfall in the pass, at this very moment.'

'Or he may have made it through before the earthquake, and be in Bologna by now.'

'Both outcomes are plausible, and many others. Do you want to go back home and explain to father that we turned back when we got delayed?'

'No, I suppose not.'

'We may arrive in Venice too late, but at least we will have tried.'

'That's true.'

'And I do so want to see Venice, don't you?'

'Yes, I do.'

'I also want to see Bologna and Padua.'

'Signor Fratteli, that lustful, papal winemaker, spoke wistfully about the food and wine in Bologna.'

'There you are, Antonio. As an apprentice winemaker, you should take every opportunity to taste new wines.'

'Bloody cheek. Have you finished in that bathtub yet?

It's my turn.'

CHAPTER TWELVE

Antonio and Maria reached Bologna, on Thursday, the first of October.

'We could keep going another hour, Maria, it's not yet dusk.'

'No, I've heard a lot about Bologna, and I want to see just a little of it before dark. Let's find an inn.' They rode slowly through the busy streets, admiring the porticoed pavements.

'It looks like they must get a lot of rain here, judging by the sheltered footways. Tell me, what exactly is it that you've heard about Bologna?' Antonio asked, as they rode into the city centre.

'First, it is the oldest university in the western world. But more importantly, in my opinion, is that they have admitted women since the thirteenth century. Women teach here too.'

'Is that rare?'

'I'll say it's rare. I think that building must be part of the university,' Maria said, studying a grand stone-built building to their left. 'Yes, it's the library. It's also supposed to be the gastronomic capital of the world. I think we shall eat well tonight, Brother.'

'There's an inn over there. Shall we try that one?' They took a room at the inn, had their horses stabled, and then went out for a stroll around the city centre. It was a bustling city with many groups of students, mostly male, but quite a few girls, too. They took a peek into the library.

'Have you ever seen so many books?'

'Never. I'm getting hungry though, I'd like to go back to the inn, and eat.' The dining room was busy, bustling with laughter and chatter. The innkeeper showed them to an empty table. There was a table of students nearby, four boys and two girls, a blonde and a brunette.

'We have minestrone soup to start, then tortellini stuffed with minced beef and cheese, and served in a capon broth. For dessert, we have a cherry tart with cream. How does that sound?'

'Amazing, I'll have that. Can we have some bread too?' Maria asked.

'Of course, signorina, and signor?'

'I'll have the same, please.' Maria glanced around the dining room. The blonde at the nearby table was looking at Antonio. She looked away when she caught Maria's gaze. 'That blonde girl fancies you, Brother. Have you seen her?'

'Yes, she's stunning. What makes you think she fancies me, though?'

'Are you joking? The way she's looking at you, of course. Haven't you noticed?'

'Well, I saw her smile, but lots of people smile.'

'What about the way she ran the tip of her tongue over her lips, as she saw you glance her way?'

'This soup's amazing. She was probably licking some soup from her lips.'

'The way she ran her fingers through her hair, when you glanced at her?'

'Perhaps it was tangled.'

'And you didn't notice her pupils dilate when you smiled at her?'

'Di what?'

'Get bigger. Oh, you're hopeless. Why don't you go over and talk to her?'

'What, while she's eating? I wouldn't want to spoil her meal. What would I say?'

'As little as possible. Smile, make eye contact. Stand with your feet wider apart than normal to show off your manliness. Puff yourself up a bit. Run your fingers through your own hair. Oh, you've missed your chance. They're getting up to leave. Why don't you just say hello?'

'I couldn't. Anyway, they have gone now. What's all this tongue and lips and eye stuff then?'

'Cecile, one of my friends, says most boys are hopeless at body language. That's the truest thing she's ever said. She says it's because God designed women to communicate with little humans who can't talk. I suppose we're just naturally better at it. But if you can bother to learn a little about it, it will help you find out which girls are interested in you, and which aren't. She says that most boys' attempts at wooing are like trying to catch fish by standing in the middle of a river, and lashing out at them with a club. Don't worry, I'll give you a few tips on our journey.'

'Why are you crying, Papa?' William asked, dropping his teddy bear. Anthony picked his small son up and hugged him as he paced around the lounge.

'I've been helping mummy peel the onions in the kitchen, that's all.'

'When are Antonio and Maria coming home, Papa?'

'I don't know, soon I hope,' he sobbed. 'Shall we talk about something else? You've never asked me who made God. Shall I tell you a story?'

'Is it the one about nothing, which one day, in the beginning, broke into opposite universes, like a credit and a debit universe?' William asked.

'Oh, I must have told you, I don't remember.'

'No, I told him,' Francesca called from the kitchen doorway. 'It was the moment I fell in love with you. You were walking in the park with a small girl. She was upset about someone in her family who had died, and you calmed her with that story. She wasn't your daughter, but I knew you'd make a wonderful father.'

'Marie de Medici. She's the queen of France now. I haven't made such a wonderful father though, have I.'

'Well, to be fair, you didn't know you were to be a father when you had to flee Florence. Of course, I wished you'd found your way back before Antonio and Maria were teenagers. But you've made up for it since.'

'I fell in love with you at the same moment, you know. Though I confess I had been in love before, or thought I had been. When I had to leave Florence, because of the duke's brother, Walsingham sent me to spy on the Spanish armada. When it was over, I was sketching the ships in the harbour from a cliff top. A silly young-girl crept up on me and frightened the life out of me. She persuaded me to sketch her, and I did try to draw her. But as she said, it looked nothing like her. I had sketched you, from memory, perfect in every detail.'

'Oh Anthony, do you still have it?'

'No. When Catherine de Medici's troops imprisoned me in Bordeaux, I lost everything.'

'Not everything. You had me and the twins, if only you'd known it.'

'Yes, if only I'd known. I could make that sketch again, from memory now, if you like.'

'Maybe, but I'd rather you continue to love me as I am, rather than as I was.'

'I see little difference. Oh why, God forgive me, did I go with Hugh and Aldobrandini? I wouldn't have met Paolo, and Maria and Antonio wouldn't be facing God knows what dangers now.' Francesca put down her kitchen knife and took off her apron and walked towards him. She took William from him and put him down.

'Why don't you go and make some sand castles in the sandpit, William. It's too nice a day to be inside.'

'All right, Mama,' William went to the door and reached up to handle, to let himself out. Francesca wrapped her arms around Anthony.

'What is he like, this Paolo?'

'Gentle and kind, yet ruthlessly intelligent.'

'What do you mean by ruthlessly intelligent?'

'I'm not sure exactly. Do you believe in the afterlife?'

'Of course, I always have, I think.'

'Well Paolo is a priest, and yet he doesn't, or at least

not in the way that I do. The way he explained it, whatever soul we have, it won't have our memories, our sight, our hearing, or our thoughts. And he isn't the only one. Cardinal Bellarmine agrees with him. He pointed out that for Christ to appear before his disciples, and speak to them, his body had to be resurrected.'

'Yes, that's right.'

'So does that mean that God will resurrect us all one day, judgement day? And what about the innocents who have been burnt? What about the long dead, who have rotted away? It all just seems so fantastical. Paolo said he would be absorbed by God, but that God is not partitioned into separate identities.'

'It may be fantastical, that's why you have to have faith, to believe it.'

'I'm sorry, Francesca, don't feel sad for me, but I think I've lost my faith on this journey. They wrote the gospels decades after Christ's death, you know, a monk told me so. And there are many more gospels than appear in the bible. A council of senior churchmen spent ages deciding which to include, and which not to include, because they were contradictory.'

'Well, I'm sure they know what's best.'

'I'm sure that they don't. These men burn other men for heresy, because they use their reason, their God-given brains, to show that the Earth revolves around the sun. The churchmen prefer to rely on an obscure verse in Genesis. Reason is fallible though, he was wrong about the tides.'

'Who was?'

'Galileo. In all other respects, he seemed immensely

clever.'

'Well, there you are then. Shall I tell you my favourite verse from the bible? Corinthians, I think it is. "Now we see but a poor reflection as in a mirror; then we shall see face to face. Now I know in part; then I shall know fully, even as I am fully known. And now these three remain: faith, hope and love. But the greatest of these is love." Love is what matters most, my darling man, and love you have given me in abundance. They will be all right, you know, Antonio and Maria. I can feel it.'

Antonio and Maria left the outskirts of Rovigo behind them, heading north. They reached a river around midday, and let the horses drink while they replenished their water pouches.

'We may as well let the horses graze a while. I've run out of carrots. What about you?' Maria asked.

'I'm out too. They certainly help us cover the miles, though. We must get some more in Monselice.' When the horses seemed sated, they mounted and continued their journey. By late afternoon, the horses seemed to be tiring again.

'There's a farm ahead on the left. I wonder if they'll sell us some carrots?' Maria suggested.

'Possibly, but we're sure to get some in Monselice, it can't be much further.'

'That's where the farm of this Gino Torelli is meant to be, isn't it?'

'Yes. But we were told to call in on the way back. I thought that catching Orlandini was the priority.'

'Well, we can kill two birds with one stone, can't we? Even better, we'll be buying at wholesale prices, not retail. Yes, the sign on the gate says Torelli Farm. Let's see.'

They rode up to the farmhouse. There was a rail that three horses were already hitched to, so they dismounted and hitched Allegro and Bellezza to one of the wheels of a cart by a barn. They were walking up a path to the farmhouse when they heard a woman scream. They stopped at once and crouched down. They edged towards a window and peeked over the sill. It was a kitchen. There were four men, and a pregnant young woman. The youngest of the men was tied to a kitchen chair. His wrists were lashed to the arms of the chair. A large man, probably in his mid-forties, was bending over the man in the chair, holding iron pincers in one hand. Another, slightly shorter man, was trying to hold the pregnant woman still, and had one hand over her mouth. The other man was standing by the door, with a sword drawn.

'I'm guessing the guy in the chair is Gino,' Maria whispered, looking around. 'There's a shovel leaning against the wall, over there. You crawl over and fetch it.' When Antonio crawled back, Maria continued. 'I'll fling open the door. You take out the swordsman with the shovel. I'll go for the one holding the woman. The other is for whichever of us gets to him first. Are you ready?'

'Yes.'

Maria slowly turned the door handle. When she felt that it wasn't locked, she flung it open. Antonio leapt through the doorway and swung the blade of the shovel into the swordsman's face as he turned towards him. The swordsman crumpled to the ground. The man holding Juliet released his grip, and his hand reached for his sword as he moved towards the intruders. He stood in front of Juliet, facing Maria and Antonio, the sword in his right hand. His left hand felt for a dagger in his belt and drew it.

'Come on then,' he leered. Juliet felt for a saucepan behind her, gripped it and swung it down as hard as she could onto the crown of the man's head. The large man dropped the pincers onto the floor and drew his own sword. He pushed past Juliet, and, raising his sword, lunged at Antonio. Before he could complete his lunge, Maria aimed a kick at his left knee, which cracked, and he fell to the ground, writhing and screaming in agony. Antonio took the sword from him and collected up the other swords and knives.

'We were hoping to buy some carrots,' Antonio explained, as he went to look at Gino. 'Here, let's get you untied. God's teeth, what have they done to you?'

'He said Pope Paul had sent them to find out the truth about Paolo Sarpi. I told him everything I knew, but he wasn't satisfied. He wanted me to say that I was sent by Paolo to murder priests by burning them. He didn't believe my denials, and he lopped off the little finger of my left hand. Juliet screamed, and then you burst in. Thanks be to God. He said he was going to lop them all off unless I talked.'

'Juliet, have you got some clean cloth? I'll bandage Gino's hand. Hold your hand up in the air above you, Gino, until we can get it treated.' Juliet went to a kitchen drawer and pulled out some cloth.

'This is clean.'

'Good. Now have you got some oregano or thyme?'

'Both, in the herb garden outside.'

'Excellent, bring me a handful of each, could you?' When Juliet came back in and handed Maria the herbs, she wrapped them up in the cloth. 'Okay, Gino, I'm going to wrap this around the end of your finger. It will stop it from becoming infected.'

'I might need some more rope,' Antonio said.

'There's some in the barn, I'll fetch it.' Gino winced.

'Thanks, Gino, I'd go, but I think it's best if I stay here until we can get these fellows trussed up.' Gino reappeared moments later with some rope. Antonio and Maria trussed up the pope's men, the man whose knee Maria had broken, screaming every few seconds. 'Sister, you'd better do something about this chap's leg.'

'Do I have to?'

'I can't see any other outcome, in which he won't die.'

'Fair enough. Find me two pieces of wood, to make splints will you.' When Antonio returned with some pieces of wood, Maria selected the best two and placed them either side of the chief inquisitor's knee, strapping them above and below the knee with the remaining cloth. 'Have you got any brandy?' Maria asked.

'We have some homemade cider-brandy,' Juliet replied, handing a small flagon to Maria.

'Okay, drink this. It'll dull the pain,' she said, offering it to the chief inquisitor.

'Could you fetch another flagon please, Juliet?' Gino asked. 'I think I need some too.'

'Of course, dear.'

'Do you intend to kill us?' the chief inquisitor gasped.

'It's an idea. But I'll give you another option,' Maria said slowly, savouring her words, 'You go back to the pope and tell him that you tortured Gino, lopped off his finger, and threatened his pregnant wife. As he wouldn't be able to work the farm, and support his wife and unborn child, without the use of his hands, you are quite certain he would have told you the whole truth. So you are certain that Gino is not involved in any plot. That will have the benefit, for you, of being true.'

'Yes, but it is not what he wants to hear.'

'Very well, I have another option for you. Why not tell the pope that a pregnant woman, a teenage girl and a teenage boy beat you up, and that's why you couldn't complete your interrogation. That also has the benefit of being true. I see you don't like that option either, so I have a third option. Why don't you go somewhere else to ply your evil trade? I'm sure there must be many kings and dukes who would pay for your services. Start out anew. You will need a more sedentary occupation in the meantime, for a few months. Have you considered writing? You could try to write your autobiography. I've got a title for you, Confessions of a Torturer. Or if looking into your own soul is too unpleasant for you, and I can see how it might be, what about a series of interviews with interesting people you've met? You could call that, In the Torturer's Chair.'

'Why are you so bloody angry? I'm only doing my job. Not everyone can be a carpenter or a stonemason. Soldiers kill men because their masters pay them to. I extract truth from men because that's what my master pays me to do, and I'm very good at it.'

'But you aren't, are you? You just said that you couldn't tell the pope that there was no plot, because that's not what he wants to hear. That may well be the truth. I happen to think it is. But it's not good enough for you. It won't make your master happy. So you keep on cutting off fingers, or whatever it is you do, until your victim breaks, and tells you whatever lies you want to hear. If you don't like any of these options, then if Gino will lend us his horse and cart, we will take you to somewhere secluded and leave you there. It's your choice. Gino, I presume you have half a dozen burly farmhands working out in the fields.'

'Yes, that's right,' Gino replied after a moment's thought.

'It's probably best you arm them well. The swords these nice men have dropped off will do for a start. Try not to be alone for a few months and ensure that Juliet is well protected too,' Antonio added.

'It looks like a couple of your farmhands are coming up to the farmhouse now,' Maria said, glancing out of the window. She went to the door, opened it and stepped outside, closing the door behind her. When they got to her, she put her finger to her lips and whispered, 'There are three of the pope's men inside. They have tortured Gino. He's alright now, just missing a little finger. How many of you are there?'

'Just us, signorina.'

'Well, they think there are six of you. I think it's best if they continue to think that. It will deter them from trying again. Mind you, the leader is not going to be able to walk for a few months. My brother and I arrived by accident and overpowered them. They are trussed up quite securely, and their leader has a broken knee. My brother and I are going to leave soon. Do you think you can deal with them?'

'Yes, we'll deal with them.'

'Good. Let's go in then.' They all went inside. 'Gino, Juliet, my brother and I are going to have to get going. I hope that your farmhands and you can cope with these villains?'

'Of course,' Gino replied, 'we really can't thank you enough. How can I repay you?'

'We did just drop in for some carrots. Two small sacks will suffice.'

CHAPTER THIRTEEN

Maria and Antonio left Mira in the first of the morning twilight on Monday, the fifth of October. It was a short ride to Mestre, and they arrived two hours later. There was a boat tied up to the quay, with men loading caskets into it.

'Can you ferry us to Saint Mark's square, sir?' Antonio asked the man who was supervising.

'We're not a ferry. See over there,' the man said, pointing across the lagoon, 'those two boats passing. The one coming towards us is the next ferry. That'll take you to Saint Marks. You'll have time to stable your horses at the inn you just passed.'

'Thank you, sir. Sister, you wait here while I go back and stable the horses. Don't let the ferry leave without me.' Maria dismounted, and Antonio led her horse back to the inn. The ferry was gliding up to the quay as he rejoined her. Half a dozen passengers climbed out, and then they boarded. There were no other passengers waiting.

'Saint Marks, is it, sir?' the helmsman asked.

'Yes please,' Antonio replied.

'Five soldi each then please.' Anthony picked the

coins out of his purse and paid.

'Can we get going, please? We're in a hurry.'

'I need a few more passengers first, sir. The next ferry won't be back for a quarter of an hour.'

'How many passengers can you carry?'

'Sixteen, at a stretch, without too much luggage.' Antonio opened his purse again and pulled out a crown. He offered it to the helmsman.

'There, that should cover it. Can we go now, please?'

'Cast off, Giorgio!' Giorgio, the crewman, released and coiled the mooring rope, then pushed the boat off the quayside with an oar. He hauled on a halyard and the sail rattled up the mast. It filled with wind, the boat heeled, and they were soon sailing briskly towards Venice.

'Isn't this marvellous? Our first taste of sailing,' Maria exclaimed, her black hair streaming in the wind. Antonio smiled.

'Yes, it is rather.' Gradually, the buildings became clearer.

'That tall tower is the campanile in Saint Mark's Square,' shouted the helmsman, as the wind strengthened, the boat heeled further, and surged towards it, 'you'll be there soon enough.'

'We hope so,' Maria called out. Twenty minutes later, they jumped ashore whilst the crewman was still making the mooring ropes fast. 'Where is the ducal palace?'

'That extensive building on the right, with the ornate colonnade,' the helmsman answered. Maria and Antonio ran towards it, crossed a bridge over a canal, and ran to the third door beyond the palace. A plaque beside the door read Fra Paolo Sarpi. Antonio knocked on the door.

He could hear footsteps approaching, and the door opened.

'What is it now?' a middle-aged woman asked.

'Is Brother Sarpi in?' Maria asked.

'He's popular today. No, he's out.'

'Where is he?'

'He left a good half an hour ago, to see a friend, if the others haven't caught up with him yet.'

'What others, signora? Please tell us, Brother Paolo is in great danger.'

'Oh heavens, three men were here ten minutes ago. They said that the doge needed to see him urgently. I told them he'd gone to visit his friend, Luigi Bonnelli, in San Marziale.'

'Did one of them have sunken eyes?'

'Now that you mention it, yes, he did. The one doing the talking, that is, what I could see of him under his hood.'

'What colour hood?'

'They were all wearing brown cloaks with their hoods up.'

'Did Paolo walk or take a gondola?' Antonio asked.

'He likes to walk, as I told the others. It helps him think, so he says.'

'Which way is it?'

'Well, the quickest way is to go back to Saint Mark's Square and head north past the Basilica. Then—'

'Come on, Brother, we'll ask as we go,' Maria shouted as she tugged his sleeve. They sprinted back to Saint Mark's Square and ran north past the cathedral. They kept jinking left and right through narrow lanes, with tightly packed buildings on each side. Eventually they reached a magnificent covered bridge over a canal, much wider than the ones that had been crossing.

'Which way to San Marziale, please, sir?' Maria gasped at a stall holder.

'That way. Keep the Grand Canal on your left. Follow the Giovanni Grisostomo across five small bridges until you reach Campo Santa Fosca. From there cross the Ponte Santa Fosca to your right, and San Marziale is dead ahead across one more small bridge.'

'Thank you, sir,' Maria shouted, breathing hard, as she and Antonio sprinted off in the direction indicated.

They had just reached Campo Santa Fosca when Antonio saw three hooded men in brown cloaks ahead of them. He grabbed Maria's arm.

'Stop! There they are! We shouldn't run, they'll hear us. Walk as briskly as you can.' As they approached Ponte Santa Fosca, they were only a few yards behind them. There was a solitary, tall, slim man in a black robe ahead of them. As the assassins followed their prey onto the bridge, there was a flash of sunlight reflected from a blade as they saw the three hooded men pull stilettos from under their cloaks.

'Now!' Antonio shouted, sprinting forwards. Antonio grabbed the hood of the assassin nearest to him, and he spun around, the thin blade in his right hand. He made a lunge at Antonio, but Antonio grabbed his wrist and pulled, twisting his body to the left and down, using the attacker's momentum to hurl him across his back and headfirst into the parapet of the bridge. Maria dealt with her target in a similar way as he turned, startled, and lunged at her. Her attacker didn't hit the parapet, but flew clean over it, into the canal beneath. The final assassin seemed stunned for a split second. Antonio saw fear in his sunken eyes, but then Orlandini ran at Sarpi, who had turned to see the commotion. Antonio dived and grasped Orlandini's left ankle. Orlandini struggled and lunged at Sarpi, falling to the ground as he did so. Sarpi's hands went to his left side, and he fell to his knees. Orlandini lost hold of the stiletto, as Sarpi fell, and the bloody blade tinkled as it hit the stone bridge. Orlandini kicked his leg violently, loosening Antonio's grip. He tried to pick up the knife again, but Maria kicked it away. Crowds gathered, keeping their distance from the fight. The assassin Antonio had thrown against the parapet, got to his feet, pushed Antonio aside, and grabbed Orlandini's arm.

'Run!' he shouted, and they sprinted off. Antonio gave chase.

'No! help me! They've wounded Paolo,' Maria called after him, 'lie down Paolo, you've been stabbed.'

'What should we do, Ma.. Sister?'

'I'm trying to think. What did father tell us of the medicine he read about in those Arabic books of the dukes? Paolo, I'm going to press on your wound and try to stem the bleeding. You put something under his head to cushion it. And get a coat or something to put under his knees. We should elevate his legs.' The surrounding crowd was growing larger and pressing in on them.

'Get back! What are you all gawping at? Fetch a

doctor!' Antonio shouted.

'You heard the man, Steffan. Run and fetch Doctor Manelli. Tell him Brother Sarpi has been stabbed,' said a woman to her young boy. The boy ran off.

'Use my coat under his knees,' a man said, taking off his coat and handing it to Anthony.

'We're going to need some cloth to make bandages. Take your shirt off and cut it into strips, Brother!'

'No, use this,' the mother said, pulling a roll of cloth from her basket. 'I was going to make some new curtains, but Brother Sarpi's need is greater than mine.' Antonio took it and bit into an edge. Then he began tearing it into long strips and passing them to Maria. She rolled one up and placed it over the wound.

'Can you sit up a tiny bit, Paolo, so that I can pass this bandage around you. Thats it, good. Left over right, right over left. Another please, Brother.' Antonio passed her another strip of cloth, and Maria secured it around the bandage.

'Thank you, angel,' Paolo whispered, staring into her eyes. 'Who are you?'

'I cannot say, Paolo. All I will say is that you impressed a stranger with your goodness, and that was enough, I hope, to save you. Pope Paul sent the assassins who attacked you. It would be much better for us if he doesn't learn of our intervention. Can you help us with that?'

'You truly are an angel. Yes, I can help you,' Paolo whispered.

'Make way! Make way!' cried a man carrying a leather bag, and pushing through the crowd. He knelt down by Sarpi and felt the pulse in his neck. 'Well, young lady, you've done all the right things. I don't want to undo your good work. How big is the wound?'

'The knife is over there, Doctor, a stiletto, very narrow.'

'Good! If it's missed his liver and kidney, he should recover. My assistant will be here in a minute with a stretcher. We'll get him back to my house and get some herbs on the wound, to prevent infection. You have done well, Signorina. Venice owes you a great debt. What is your name?'

'Angelica. You can call me Angelica.'

'You must be Angelica's brother, young man. What's your name?'

'William,' Antonio answered after a slight hesitation. A gangly looking boy pushed his way through the crowd, hauling two wooden poles with a sheet of canvas between them.

'Lay the stretcher down beside him, Mario. Angelica, could you and William help us lift Brother Paolo onto the stretcher, please?' This they did together. 'Good. Now, if Mario takes one end, and William takes the other, I will lead the way back to my house. Make way, make way!' The crowds parted and minutes later, they arrived at a large, three-story house. Doctor Manelli opened the door and led them down a corridor. 'Bring him in here.' he said, opening a door onto a large, airy room. Maria and Antonio tried to manoeuvre the stretcher through the doorway.

'I'll get that,' Maria said, lifting a small table and vase of flowers out of the way.

'Put him down beside the bed. Good. Now, Mario, you take his legs and if William takes his arms, could you Angelica help me support his body? On the count of three, we will all lift. Ready? One, two, three, there. Are you all right, Paolo?' Paolo winced and nodded. 'I'm going to select some herbs, then I will remove the dressing that Angelica has applied, and have a look at your wound. Then I will apply a new dressing with a poultice to prevent infection.' Doctor Manelli went to some shelves which supported a few dozen labelled glass jars with herbs, flower petals and coloured powders. He selected four jars and spooned some of the contents into a mortar on the desk under the shelves. He pounded them with a pestle. Then he opened a desk drawer and took out some cloth and binding. He spooned the mixture onto the cloth and folded it. Then he came back to the bed. 'Paolo, I'm going to take your dressing off now. We'll have to remove your robe too. It's going to hurt I'm afraid.' He selected a knife from his desk and cut the bandage which Maria had applied. He removed the blood-soaked dressing. Blood on the robe had spread out to about a six-inch radius from the wound, but had coagulated. 'The least painful way is if I cut your robe. Is that all right, Paolo?' Paolo nodded. 'You should leave the room, Angelica.'

'If Paolo doesn't mind, I'd like to stay. I hope you're not offended, Doctor, but in a silly way, I feel as if he's my patient too.'

'I have no doubt you saved his life, so is it all right with you, Paolo, if Angelica stays?' Paolo nodded, and Doctor Manelli gently cut away his robe. He and Mario rolled Paolo onto his unwounded side, and with a few more cuts, pulled his robe free in tatters. They rolled Paolo onto his back again. Doctor Manelli took a blanket from a box at the bottom of the bed and spread it over Paolo's legs and waist. Then he examined the wound, which was bleeding again. 'I think the knife has missed the vital organs. You are lucky that Angelica and William were around. You have lost a lot of blood, but they made a fine job of stemming the bleeding and maintaining the blood flow to your heart. I am hopeful that you will make a full recovery. You will need to rest, and we will get you some hot broth to speed your recovery.'

'Doctor Manelli, would you mind if we stay around for a few days? We would like to be sure that Paolo is recovering well,' Maria asked.

'Of course not. From your accent, you aren't Venetian. Where are you from?'

'We're from—'

'We're from Florence,' Maria interrupted Antonio.

'Yes, I thought that was a Florentine accent. I'm afraid I don't have room for you here, but there is a pleasant inn around the corner. It's clean and reasonably priced.'

Antonio and Maria visited Paolo for the next few days. They could see he was recovering well, able to sit up in bed, and was eating and drinking enough to satisfy Doctor Manelli. On Thursday, the eighth of October, they were sitting beside his bed talking with him.

'We are pleased to see you are recovering so well. We shall have to return home now, Paolo,' Maria said.

'So soon? I shall pray for your safe journey. You will

stay just a little longer, I hope. What time is it?'

'I heard the bells chime midday, perhaps ten minutes ago,' Antonio answered.

'Then please wait, just a few minutes more. I am expecting a visitor. I'd like you to meet him,' Paolo implored. Antonio and Maria exchanged glances.

'No, we really should go,' Maria said, squeezing Paolo's hand. There was a knock on the door. Doctor Manelli went and opened the door.

'Your Serenity, welcome to my humble house and surgery. He is in here. Doctor Manelli returned, followed by a middle-aged man, resplendent in silk robes, with a gold chain hung around his neck. He was followed by two younger, armed men. Antonio and Maria tensed, ready to fight if necessary.

'My lord, this is an honour,' Paolo said, wriggling to sit more upright in bed.

'I was distressed to hear of the violent attack on you, Paolo. When I heard they had taken you to Doctor Manelli, I knew you were in safe hands. I also heard of the young brother and sister who beat off your attackers. Are these that heroic pair?'

'Indeed they are, my lord. May I introduce Angelica and William? This is the doge.'

'Venice is deeply grateful to you both. Without your prompt and exceptional intervention, Venice would have lost our greatest mind and advocate. Where and what family are you from?'

'If I may intercede, my lord. They are from outside Venice, and live under papal rule. If Pope Paul learnt of their intervention on my behalf, then they and their family would not be safe.'

'So be it then. How do you know that Pope Paul was responsible?'

'The man who stabbed me, my lord. As he lunged at me he screamed, "this is from Pope Paul." I could see in his eyes, he spoke the truth.'

'I see, though I am unsure I see the same in your eyes, Paolo. But you are a wise councillor. I will let it rest. The purses please, Alfredo.' One bodyguard handed the doge two silk-purses. 'William and Angelica, please accept these purses as a small token of the gratitude of Venice.'

'Thank you, my lord,' they said, Antonio bowing and Maria curtseying. 'Were the assassins caught, my lord?' Maria asked.

'Unfortunately not. They seem to have fled the city. We will assign a bodyguard to ensure that Paolo is protected in the future. Such a villainous attack will not be unexpected and unguarded against in the future. But for now, I must be going.' When the doge and his guards had left, Maria opened her purse and counted the gold coins.

'Twenty ten-ducat coins,' she exclaimed.

'At last I know my true worth,' Paolo laughed, 'what an unpleasant way to find out.'

'Two hundred ducats. I wonder if that's enough to buy a boat?' Maria pondered aloud.

'It depends how big a boat you're thinking of. It will buy three years' work of a skilled craftsman. I don't know the price of oak, rope, or the other materials required,' Doctor Manelli answered.

CHAPTER FOURTEEN

Maria and Antonio were riding south west, towards Padua on the first leg of the journey home. Antonio kept glancing at his sister, but she seemed deep in thought.

'What's on your mind, Maria?'

'How much money do we make a year from the vineyard?'

'That's hard to say. Last year we made only about a hundred ducats, after expenses and taxes. But it was only our first year of operation. Signor Fratteli had some excellent advice, about how we can improve the quality of our wine, and achieve a higher price for it. He thought we might earn, perhaps three, or even four hundred ducats a year. Father wants to buy a still and make brandy. I have some ideas too. If I rode around the local towns, selling our wine by the barrel, directly to inns and taverns, I should be able to get a higher price for it than selling to the wine merchants. Perhaps we could grow to six hundred ducats a year. From what Doctor Manelli was saying, that's what eight skilled craftsmen could earn. Not bad, eh?'

'Well, in two weeks, call it three weeks, by the time

we get home, we've made four hundred ducats. In a month, father and Hugh made four thousand ducats, between them, for catching a couple of art thieves.'

'Don't forget that mother has her eye on a chunk of father's two thousand for your dowry.'

'I told her, I'm not for sale.'

'Don't you want to marry, and have a family?'

'I might, but if I do, it will be for love, not money, and I want to see the world first. I might fall in love with a poor man, so it's important that I make a fortune of my own first, while I can. Perhaps we could have a sideline in solving crimes for wealthy men.'

'What wealthy men do you have in mind?'

'Well, the doge seems to be a fan. I'm sure he might have some special missions that we could help him with, from time to time.'

'The pope pays better.'

'The pope was employing father and Hugh to do what they did. The doge was giving us a gesture of thanks, a gratuity after the fact. It's a different matter altogether. Father has taught us some precious skills, but I think he can teach us some more.'

'Such as what, Maria?'

'He hasn't taught us how to pick locks yet, has he?'

'I think mother might object to that.'

'Or how he broke the Spanish ciphers.'

'Don't forget he made several fortunes and lost them again; or that he spent several years in prison and thought he was sure to be executed.'

'So we learn from his mistakes, as well as his successes.'

'The pope, and Cardinal Aldobrandini sought father's help for catching those art thieves. If they have further needs, they may ask him again. We could help him.'

'Yes, you have a point. But I don't feel very inclined to serving the pope after he sent assassins to kill Paolo.'

'He pays well, and he's within a day's ride. He's an established client of father's, who has served him well. The doge is ten days' ride from Frascati. The Duke of Tuscany is five or six. How do you know the doge doesn't also pay assassins to do his dirty work? Or that the Duke of Tuscany, or any of the other dukes, don't?'

'I don't, you're right. But I draw the line at killing anyone, unless they're trying to kill me.'

'I'm glad to hear it.'

Antonio and Maria arrived back in Bologna on Sunday, the eleventh of October. They went directly to the inn that they had stayed in on their way to Venice and took a twin room.

'We have a couple of hours before dinner, Antonio, so I suggest we work on your body language. I'll pretend to be that gorgeous girl at the adjoining table. You sit on the edge of your bed, and I'll sit on the chair by the window, opposite the fire. Now, I'll flirt with you, and you try to respond.' Maria glanced at Antonio, and ran her fingers through her hair. 'It would help if you glanced at me occasionally. How can you notice what I'm doing if you stare at the wall?'

'All right, I'll try.' Maria ran her fingers through her hair again, as Antonio glanced at her.

'Good, now hold my eye contact, and preen yourself a

little. No, don't stroke your beard. That shows you're thinking. It's not about thinking, it's animal, primeval. Run your fingers through your hair. There, that's better!'

'Am I supposed to see your eyes dissipating?'

'Dilating, getting a little bigger. I can't do that. You're my brother. I can act the other things, but not that. Right, so we've established that I'm interested in you, and you've responded. We spend a little time smiling, exchanging glances, preening. Now you get up and walk over to me. Puff yourself up a bit, widen your stance. I stand up as well. Now what do you notice?'

'You're standing a bit odd.'

'Well, in what way odd?'

'You've thrust your right hip towards me, a little, and your right shoulder is higher than your left.'

'Very good, and what do you notice? Where does it draw your eye?'

'Well, your, er, your groin and your breasts. Is it the fire? I'm feeling hot.'

'Yes, and that's the idea. Get the message?'

'This is gross!'

'Only because I'm your sister. It will feel much more natural with the blonde, I promise you.'

'So when do I start talking, and what do I say?'

'Well, I would say it doesn't matter much, all the real talking is in the body language. But it would be best to avoid saying you're standing a bit odd. Try something like, I was hoping I'd see you here again. Or, do you come here often? That's a very pretty dress you're wearing. Be complimentary, ask her name. Be open and honest, although it would be best to avoid talking about foiling the pope's assassination attempt. We'll do a bit more practice.' They had just started again when there was a knock at the door. Antonio opened the door and the innkeeper and his assistant were there with a tin bath tub.

'We've brought up the bath you ordered, sir.'

'Yes thank you, bring it in.' They placed the tub on the floor in front of the fire and poured in a jug of steaming water.

'We'll run up a few more jugs, then leave you to it. Just let us know when you've finished, and we'll collect the tub.'

'Thank you,' Antonio said, leaving the door ajar.

'You take the first bath, Antonio. In the circumstances, it's better if you have the clean water. I'll go down to the bar and have a drink, and see if there's any sign of the blonde. I'll give you half an hour, then we can swap over.'

When Maria had finished her bath, she dried herself and got dressed. Then she went down and joined Antonio. They told the innkeeper that they were ready to eat and asked for the same table they'd had the last time. They enjoyed their meal, and had a second flagon of wine, but the dining room was emptying.

'It looks like she's not coming, Maria.'

'Yes, but don't despair. It's Sunday, and we saw her on Monday evening. Perhaps she'll come tomorrow evening. It might be a regular fixture. Anyway, it'll give us a chance to do some clothes shopping. All this courting advice, and taking a bath, will be enhanced if we get you some clean, nice clothes. Mine are looking rather bedraggled too. We won't go mad, but we can afford something a little more fetching. First thing after breakfast, we'll find a tailor and see what he can do for us.'

After breakfast, they explored the city again and found a tailor's shop. They went inside. It was quite a long, narrow shop. There were dolls on a long shelf down one wall, displaying miniatures of the current fashions for both men and women. There were two doors on the wall opposite, and another door at the end of the shop, opposite the door from the street.

'How can I help you, signor, signorina?'

'We have been on the road for many days, and need new clothes,' Antonio explained.

'Yes, so I see. I will take your measurements, signor, and my wife will measure you, signorina. While I fetch my wife, please look at the figures, so that we may get an idea of what you are looking for.'

'How long will it take to make something?' Maria asked.

'Not more than a week, or two, depending on the complexity of your chosen garments.'

'I'm afraid my brother and I are looking for something to wear this evening. Do you have something already made that you could alter, perhaps?' The tailor walked around each of them in turn, studying them from head to toe.

'Yes, I have something. I might have to put a dart in the back of the coat, signor has quite broad shoulders. And I might have to take the waist in a little on some breeches. I think I have the perfect thing for you, signorina. It has been waiting for you, you have the perfect figure. I apologise. I make you blush. But really, I know perfection when I see it, and I see it now. Please take a seat while I get them.' The tailor disappeared into another room at the back of the shop, where they glimpsed three or four seamstresses hard at work. He reappeared a few minutes later, with a coat, breeches, shirt and stockings, over one arm. In his free hand, he carried a small ball of twine and a piece of chalk. Behind him came a woman with a dress, stockings, and some petticoats. 'If, signor would like to follow me, and signorina go with my wife, we will see what we can do.' The tailor led Antonio through one of the doors, opposite the shelf with the dolls, and his wife led Maria through the other. Antonio found himself in a fitting room. The tailor asked him to undress, and he did so, placing his old clothes over the back of a chair. He put on the breeches, which were a little loose at the waist. 'Excuse me, signor,' the tailor said as he pulled the waist tight and made a mark with the chalk. He also ran the twine around Antonio's waist and cut it with a pair of scissors. 'The length is just right. Could you try the stockings on, signor? Yes, they fit well and will lace up nicely. The coat will require the most work. If you could try that on, signor, as I thought. Take it off again, please. Now lift your arms.' He took another piece of twine and ran it around Antonio's chest under his arms. 'Thank you, signor, you can relax now. I have all the measurements I need.' The tailor left the fitting room, and Antonio dressed in his old clothes again. As he left the fitting room, Maria was doing the same. The tailor was in quiet conversation with his wife. 'Signor, signorina, we can have these garments ready for you to collect after lunch. I trust that is satisfactory?'

'Yes, most satisfactory. What will they cost?' Maria asked.

'Well, they are fine garments. I trust you agree. Two ducats for signorina's and one ducat for signor's.'

'That's rather more than I was expecting,' said Maria, 'that's fifteen days' skilled work.'

'We may be only a few hours altering them, signorina, but much work has already gone into them. Then there is the material, the finest silk, and English wool. They will set signorina's beautiful figure off perfectly.'

'Would you take two ducats for both?' Maria asked.

'Three ducats, signorina.'

'Very well, pay the man, Brother.'

'Why me, Sister? Your outfit is the most expensive.'

'And why do we need new clothes? Who do you hope to impress?' Antonio opened his purse and took out three ducats.

Maria had just finished her main course when she saw the inn door open and the blonde girl enter. The brunette followed her, together with the same four boys as the last time she had seen them.

'She's just arrived, Antonio. I've done all I can. It's up to you now. I'm going to skip dessert and leave her to you. I'll just make certain she gets a good look at me before I go.'

'Why?'

'So that she knows I'm your sister, and not your

girlfriend, of course.'

'Where will you be?'

'I think I'll go for a walk and see what Bologna is like at night. I'll see you in the room later, perhaps.' Maria got up and walked past the new arrivals to the door. She smiled at the blonde, who smiled back. There was light rain falling, so she crossed the cobbled street to get under the portico on the other side. She followed the portico as far as a plaza, in which there were two tall towers. A cacophony of youthful voices, arguing and laughing, rang out from several taverns around the plaza. She entered a church and sat at the back for a while, admiring the paintings. A choir started singing. She found the peaceful harmony soothing. Then she thought about the pope who had sent assassins to murder Paolo, and Cardinal Aldobrandini, who had plotted it. She got up, left the church, and walked back to the inn. She looked around, but Antonio, the blonde, and her friends had gone. She went up to their room and went to bed. Church bells had just finished striking midnight when the door opened and Antonio came in.

'Well, how did it go?' she whispered.

'She's nothing short of a goddess,' Antonio replied, with a faraway look and a smile on his face.

'Does she have a name?'

'Greta.'

'And where did you go? You weren't downstairs when I got back from my walk.'

'One of the boys, I didn't get their names, wanted to move on to another tavern. Greta asked me to come with them. He didn't seem too pleased, but we went along. The boy started a drinking contest in the next tavern, and Greta suggested we slip out and go for a walk instead. We must have walked miles.'

'Just walking?'

'Well, talking too. She's in her first year of studying medicine. Her father's a doctor, in a small town near Turin. The mountains sound wonderful. She wants to show them to me one day.'

'Well that's encouraging.'

'When we got back to the university, she kissed me goodnight.'

'Anything else?'

'She asked me if I'd like to go to the theatre with her, tomorrow.'

'That sounds very encouraging.'

'Her skin is so soft, and her lips, they, I don't know how to describe them, and her eyes are so blue. They dissipate beautifully.'

'Dilate, I get the picture. I guess you'll be staying a few days in Bologna. I'll head back home tomorrow and leave you to it.'

'On your own. Will you be all right?'

'Of course I'll be all right. Have you any idea when you might come home?'

'No.'

Anthony was pacing the floor of the drawing room.

'I had hoped they might be back home by now, darling.'

'I know, I'm worried too, of course. But wearing out the floorboards won't bring them back. They might take their time riding home. You know what Maria is like, she'll want to see the sights. Venice, my oh my, what I would give to see Venice.'

'You've never said so. We can go to Venice if you like. Antonio and Maria will be able to look after the vineyard now. We could get away for a month or so, except at harvest time.'

'They'll pass through Padua and Bologna. They'll want to see Florence again, I expect, see their childhood haunts and friends. They might even—' Francesca was interrupted by the door opening.

'Hello, Mother, Father.'

'Oh thank the lord! Where's Antonio, is he putting away the horses?'

'No, I put Allegro away. I rode home alone, from Bologna.'

'Why? What's happened to him? Is he hurt?' Anthony asked, startled.

'Relax, he's fine.'

'What's he thinking, to let you ride home alone from Bologna? A young, beautiful girl on her own, on the road. I dread to think what might have happened,' Francesca spluttered.

'He's fallen in love with a medical student in Bologna. He staying there for a few days.'

'What?' Anthony exclaimed. 'I never dreamt. He didn't say, well, I didn't ask. I mean, I've known a few. Anthony Bacon was a bit that way, well, quite a bit that way, actually. We've never had that sort of thing in the family though, have you darling?' he asked, turning to Francesca.

'Honestly, Father! She's a girl. Women have been studying at Bologna for over three centuries now.'

'Oh, I see. What's she like?'

'Beautiful, and blonde. Her name's Gretta. She's from a small town in the alps, near Turin. Her father is a doctor, and she wants to follow him into medicine.'

'A doctor would be a good catch for Antonio, don't you think, Anthony?' Francesca said.

'Yes, I suppose so.'

'Were there any nice-looking boys, dear? Doctors, lawyers, did anyone take your fancy?' Francesca asked.

'No, I'm going to marry a sea captain. You've taught us a lot of things, Father, very useful things. Can you teach me to sail?'

'Well I could, I suppose, but we don't have a boat.'

'Can't we buy a boat now? I have twenty ducats left from what Hugh gave us. And you made loads from your mission, didn't you?'

'Perhaps, but where would we keep it?'

'How about at the mouth of the Tiber, Ostia perhaps?'

'Yes, that's possible.'

'You've always told such wonderful stories about your time at sea. And surfing across the lagoon to Venice, under sail, has sold it to me.'

'I will not promise anything, but we'll see.'

'Do you think Cardinal Aldobrandini might have some more missions for you in the future?' Maria asked, curling her hair in her fingers.

'Over my dead body,' Francesca said.

'Yes, my darling. Anyway, I think I've taken enough knocks. I'm not as young as I was, and it takes longer to heal. Now don't keep us in suspense. What happened? Is Paolo all right?'

'Yes, we ended up arriving at Paolo's house, about ten minutes after Orlandini and two others. They must have been delayed by the same earthquake as we were. Paolo's housekeeper told us where Paolo was going, so we chased through the streets after him. Just as we were approaching a bridge, we saw him and the three villains approaching him. They pulled out knives, but Antonio managed to throw one of them into the bridge parapet, head first. I threw the second over the bridge into the canal, and the third made a lunge at Paolo, just as Antonio dived at his ankle. Unfortunately, his stiletto still pierced Paolo's side, but not very deeply. Antonio had taken most of the energy from the lunge. The last villain ran away, so I bandaged Paolo's wound and elevated his legs whilst somebody in the crowd summoned a doctor. We didn't leave until we were sure of his recovery, and the doge is going to ensure he has a bodyguard in the future.'

'Good lord. You were taking in what I told you of the Arabic medicine book.'

'Yes, of course, and I'd like you to teach me some more things, Father.'

'I'm not sure I can teach you anything. You and your brother have defeated three villains, whilst I, with the help of three others, at times more, defeated two.'

'Oh, actually, it was six villains. We were running low on carrots for the horses, as we were riding north from Ferrara. Hugh had asked us to look in on a Gino Torelli, on the way back, but as we were passing, we thought we would see if he was all right, and get some carrots at the same time. Well, there were three of the pope's men there, and they had just chopped off Gino's little finger. So we burst in. Antonio smashed one in the head with a shovel, Juliet cracked another over the head with a saucepan, and I took out the boss with one of those kicks to the knee. I know you said only to do that in extreme circumstances, and if they outnumbered us, but we were outnumbered, sort of, as they'd tied Gino up, and his wife was pregnant.'

'Well, I'm speechless,' Anthony gasped. 'I'm so glad that you saved Gino, though. What happened to the pope's inquisitor and his men?'

'I don't know. We had to leave to race to Venice. We left them disarmed and trussed up. Gino's farmhands had just returned, and we convinced the villains that there were another four farmhands still working in the fields. We wanted to dissuade them from trying again.'

'I'm not sure I would have thought of that. Where did you get your brains?'

'From me,' Francesca cut in. 'I only wish she'd inherited a bit more of me, like a sense of self preservation. A little fear isn't such a bad thing. Why can't you find a nice young man and settle down?'

'Oh, Mother. It's been fun. I am rather hungry after the journey though. Is there any chance of something to eat?'

'Of course, I'll make your favourite,' Francesca said, going into the kitchen.

'Do you think there is any chance of Pope Paul or Aldobrandini tracing you back here?' Anthony whispered.

'I don't think so. We have always called each other

brother and sister, and used assumed names where necessary.'

'That was good thinking. But what about the inquisitor and his men? If they return to Rome, and describe you and Antonio, to either Pope Paul or Aldobrandini, they may realise it was you.'

'I don't think they will return to Rome, Papa. They won't want to admit to their failure, particularly at the hands of a girl.'

'What if Orlandini returns to Rome, and describes you both?'

'I don't think he will either, Papa, for the same reason. Anyway, while Mother's in the kitchen, I haven't heard how you and Hugh got on. All I know is that your mission was successful, and that Aldobrandini sent Rotilio Orlandini to assassinate Paolo Sarpi, who you and Hugh both liked. We found him a delightful man too.'

'Well, it's a long story. Someone was murdering priests and burning them in their own churches, on saint's days. A bund of earth surrounded the bodies. It reminded me of a story I heard about a professor named Galileo who believes that the Earth revolves around the sun, which is heresy officially. So we set about interviewing students and past students of his. There was an Englishman named Mark Brown amongst them, an artist. He seemed a most unlikely suspect, but we discovered that he was the illegitimate son of a man called Giordano Bruno, who was burnt by the church for the heresy of believing this sun and Earth thing. Actually, that wasn't the real reason he was burnt. But the son thought so, and set about avenging the father he had never known. It makes you wonder who the real criminals are, doesn't it? He was shot through the head, as he was about to burn me.'

'My god!'

'His father seems to have been a very intelligent man, whose motive was to bring peace between the Protestants and Catholics, and between nations. Not much of a crime, is it?'

'No, Father.'

'I tracked down, and brought about the death of his only child, for the grand sum of two thousand ducats.'

'You probably saved the lives of many innocent priests.'

'I'm no longer sure there are many innocent priests.'

'Well, I broke the knee of a torturer for a bag of carrots. I really rather enjoyed it.'

'What have I unleashed on the world?' Anthony asked, wrapping his arms around Maria. 'Thank you.'

'For what, Father?'

'For saving the lives of both Gino and Paolo. They would have been on my conscience, if you had not.'

'Why? It was Pope Paul and Cardinal Aldobrandini that threatened them.'

'And I, unwittingly and unintentionally, incriminated them. So thank you.'

'Perhaps you should thank Hugh.'

'And I will, if your mother gives me the chance.'

'If you do want to thank me, Papa, there are a few more things Antonio and I think you can teach us. You haven't taught us yet how to pick locks, and neither have you told us how you broke the Spanish ciphers. You must have been very clever to do that, Papa.'

AFTERWORD

There is a statue of Paolo Sarpi in Campo Santa Fosca Square, Venice. It was commissioned by the people of Venice, sculpted by Emilio Marsili, and erected in 1892 to mark the place where one of the city's greatest sons survived an assassination attempt on the nearby bridge. Pope Paul V hired a defrocked priest, by the name of Rotilio Orlandini, and his brother-in-law, to kill Sarpi for the sum of eight thousand crowns. On the fifth of October 1607, Sarpi was attacked and stabbed on the bridge, but he survived and lived a full and active life until his death on the fifteenth of January 1623, at the age of seventy.

Giordano Bruno was burnt on the seventeenth of February 1600 in Campo dei Fiori, Rome, following a trial lasting eight years. Cardinal Bellarmine led his trial, in which the future Pope Paul also sat in judgement. There is evidence to suggest that Bruno's diplomacy between Henry III of France and Queen Elizabeth I was the real cause of his trial and execution. Bruno was an adherent of the Copernican theory of the universe, also suggesting that there were numerous other inhabited planets. His greatest wish, expressed through his many books, was a reconciliation of the fragmented church, and a return to the values of the early Christian community.

Galileo Galilei famously fought his own long-running battle with the church over the Copernican model of the solar system. He considered that his model of the tides proved beyond doubt that the Earth rotated and orbited the sun. There was no place in Galileo's model for the moon.

Sir Anthony Standen did spy for Francis Walsingham, and fed back more detailed intelligence on the Spanish Armada than Walsingham could have dreamt of. My fictionalised account of his life is published as The Spy who Sank the Armada. It remains true to the vast majority of the known facts of Standen's life, and the history of the times, whilst telling, I hope, an entertaining tale. It is my intention, God willing, to tell more stories of the Standen clan, set against the backdrop of history. I hope you enjoy reading them as much as I enjoy researching and writing them. Please leave a review, they are very helpful.

ABOUT THE AUTHOR

David V.S. West was educated at St. Edmund Hall, Oxford, where he took a B.A. in Engineering Science. During a career in engineering and project management he was commissioned by Gower Publishing to write a book on Project Sponsorship. This led him to study creative writing with the Open University, and a new career as a writer. The Spy who Sank the Armada is the first novel in the series The Sir Anthony Standen Adventures. He lives in Wiltshire.

Printed in Great Britain
by Amazon